KU-764-675

# Flying Colours

## Heather Graves

ROBERT HALE · LONDON

© Heather Graves 2005
First published in Great Britain 2005

ISBN 0 7090 7855 2

Robert Hale Limited
Clerkenwell House
Clerkenwell Green
London EC1R 0HT

The right of Heather Graves to be identified as
author of this work has been asserted by her
in accordance with the Copyright, Designs and
Patents Act 1988.

2 4 6 8 10 9 7 5 3 1

| CROYDON LIBRARIES | |
|---|---|
| 15019904113 | |
| HJ | 23/01/2006 |
| F | £17.99 |
| | |

Typeset in 12/17pt Palatino
by Derek Doyle & Associates, Shaw Heath.
Printed in Great Britain by
St Edmundsbury Press, Bury St Edmunds, Suffolk.
Bound by Woolnough Bookbinding Limited.

# Flying Colours

# CHAPTER ONE

T HE horse flung up his head as they waited inside the barriers for the gates to spring open and the race to begin. Corey tried to settle him, murmuring encouragement but the champion was restless, all too aware of his change in rider and the unaccustomed feel of a girl's hands on his reins. Hers was a lighter touch than that of Ray Mercer, who usually rode him – presently cursing his luck as he lay in the back of an ambulance taking him from the track with a broken leg. A collision and fall in the previous event had knocked him out of the feature race, cheating him of his ride on the favoured Pirate King.

The girl was nervous too, rushed into her colours at the last minute to replace a senior rider in a race that could make or break her career. Pirate King wasn't an easy ride at the best of times, known to be skittish in the barriers and having a mind of his own during the course of a race. Tony Mackintosh, his trainer, had warned her of some of Pirate's idiosyncrasies but she had to be up and riding towards the start before he could tell her how to deal with them.

There was no time for further thought. The gates flew open and the field was on its way. From her outside position in the barrier she had two choices. She could either ride around everyone to take up the running or stay out of trouble at the rear of the field, relying on Pirate's almost legendary turn of speed to overtake his rivals in the closing stages of the race. The horse made the choice for her, settling into a comfortable stride at the rear, saving his energy for later. Thus they travelled without event. But as they rounded the turn and entered the straight, the roar of the excited crowd seemed to reach out towards her as a single organism, willing her to let the horse have his head and win. She encouraged him to speed up, showing him the whip before deciding whether to use it or not.

Wrong move. At the sight of the whip, Pirate broke his stride and skittered sideways. Fortunately, no one was in his way. Hands and heels, then. That seemed to meet with his approval. Setting his ears back, Pirate lifted his game and started around the field, overtaking them one by one. She could feel the crowd with her, roaring encouragement until there was only one horse, one lightweight outsider in the way of victory. But the post was coming up too quickly and as she thundered past the other horse, she knew she was seconds too late. Even before the course announcer confirmed it, the concerted groan of disappointment from the crowd told her she had lost. She felt her cheeks burn and she bit her bottom lip savagely in the hope that pain would drive the tears of disappointment from her eyes. Television cameras would be watching her every move and it would be most unprofessional to weep.

'Well done, kid.' One of the older jockeys called out gruffly as he rode back to the mounting yard beside her. 'Second is fair enough on that great brute. Has a mind of his own.'

'You can say that again,' she said, attempting a smile and hoping she didn't look quite as miserable and defeated as she felt. There was still the weighing in and the horse's connections to be faced. What would Tony have to say? Surely, he would regret having given her this chance in a featured race?

While the winners celebrated noisily nearby, she faced up to Tony and Pirate's owner, a tall, imposing figure of a man in an elegant, dark blue suit. With a shock of unruly black hair and unusually pale blue eyes, he would have been handsome enough to be a film star were it not for the haunted expression in his eyes and a number of little frown lines between his eyebrows, caused by sadness or ill temper, she didn't know which. It occurred to her that Pirate King and his owner might have something in common but even that thought couldn't make her smile.

'I'm so sorry, Tony.' She tried not to meet the trainer's gaze as she dismounted and freed Pirate from her saddle. 'I did my best.'

'I know you did, Corey. Thanks.' Tony patted her shoulder and smiled, taking control of Pirate who was dancing sideways, still showing no signs of weariness and getting ready to play up again. 'Second was a pretty good effort, given the circumstances—'

'A good effort?' the other man interrupted, almost snorting with indignation. He had that unusually strong

7

Australian accent, common to many born of Greek or Italian parents. 'He lost us the race.' He turned to Corey, eyes sparkling with indignation. 'I saw what you were doing out there, letting the horse dictate the terms. Why the hell didn't you use the whip?'

'Excuse me?' Corey paused and stared at him, unused to having her riding style criticized. The man stared back, only now realizing she was a girl.

'Corey – this is Mario Antonello – Pirate's new owner,' Tony broke in quickly in the hope of heading off trouble. She nodded briefly, acknowledging the introduction as she turned away, not trusting herself to speak.

'When you told me you were putting a Corey O'Brien on Pirate – I thought you would be hiring a boy.' Mario chose his words carefully, making sure she would hear. 'I would never have let you entrust this valuable animal to an immature, inexperienced girl.'

Corey felt her heart step up its beat and her cheeks burned with fury at the man's arrogance. She could understand his disappointment but it was no more acute than her own. She had done the best she could with a difficult horse and his unjust criticism was making her angry.

'Cut along and weigh in, Corey, they'll be waiting for you.' Tony gave her a meaningful look before she could draw breath to speak. Clearly, he didn't want her to say anything she might regret. 'We'll talk again in a while.'

As she left, pulling off her jockey's helmet, she could hear them continuing the argument behind her.

'I don't disapprove of girl riders entirely – they're OK for track work,' the Italian was saying. 'I know everyone's talk-

8

ing equality these days but women are never as strong as they think they are. And to expect a girl to hold her own and compete in a major race—'

'Mario, if we're going to work together, you must learn to trust my judgment. Corey's one of the best and she knows what she's doing. She comes from a well-known racing family – practically born at the track. If anything she's a more intuitive rider than Mercer and with more feeling for the horse.'

'Fine. But she wasn't there to act as nursemaid for the horse. She was supposed to make him win.'

'No such thing as a certainty in racing, Mario.' Tony was determinedly cheerful but Corey waited to hear no more, all too aware of the Italian's burning gaze on her back as she made her way back to scale.

Mario watched her leave, shoulders taut, her slight figure provocative in the tight-fitting jockey's pants. What had got into him? Why had he been so hard on her? He didn't usually fly off the handle like that. Perhaps because she reminded him too much of Rina? She even walked with the same cocky determination; the same love of dangerous sports.

Born within a week of each other, he and Rina had grown up as childhood sweethearts. They had spent all their school holidays together and she had always loved challenging him to feats of daring.

'Race you down to the beach, Mario!' she would cry, sliding and stumbling down an impossible cliff face, not caring if she grazed hands or knees. 'I can climb that tree faster than you can!' And more often than not, she could and she did, while he lumbered behind, awkward in his early teens and growing too fast into his young man's body. And as they grew older, it was inevitable that they should fall in love.

At first, his parents had been indulgent, smiling at the attachment, expecting him to grow out of it. The smiles soon faded when he didn't. He could still remember the day he stood up to his father, Rina holding fast to his hand.

'We want to be married.' He made the announcement, waiting for the storm to break over their heads.

Unwilling to take them seriously, his father mocked him, trying to laugh it off.

'Married? Don't be ridiculous – what do you know of marriage? A boy, not yet eighteen – scarcely able to grow a beard.'

'Papa, we're serious. Don't laugh at us.'

'I know, I know. But Mario, think about it. This is your cousin. My sister's child.' His father was no longer smiling. 'Cousins don't marry – not without a special dispensation.'

'Then we'll get one.'

'Let me finish,' his father glowered, unused to defiance. 'To complete your education, I want to send you to college in Italy. I need a man of business to inherit my company, not a young man bowed down with the responsibilities of a wife and too many children.' Struck by an unpleasant thought, for the first time his father looked concerned. 'I hope this isn't because you're already—?'

'No.' Mario snapped. 'Not that we didn't think of pretending to be.'

'Uncle Guido, I love Mario.' Rina said softly. 'I wouldn't

10

trap him like that.'

'I'm happy to hear it.' Mario's father didn't trouble to hide his relief. 'This – this puppy love has grown out of too much time spent in each other's company, excluding other friends. I want to see if this love of yours can survive if you are apart.'

It didn't. But not for the reasons either of them expected.

And now, right out of the blue, comes another Rina; a girl jockey riding into his life, reviving old memories and shocking him. Of course her eyes were a different colour and when he looked into her face, she wasn't like Rina at all. But that first impression had shaken him; the way she carried herself, fixing him with that same direct look, was so like his cousin, it was uncanny. He wasn't usually so volatile and short-tempered – usually he left that to his father – but the disappointment of losing the race and the shock of meeting her made him lash out. She had been upset and it was unfair, Tony had pointed that out already. Somehow he must find a way to make it up to her.

Tony waylaid Corey as she emerged from the changing room, getting ready to leave. She had no further engagements that day.

'Thanks again, kiddo.' He fell in beside her on the way to the car park. 'Take no notice of Mario. He's just a sore loser because he's new to the game. Thinks racing's the same as any other business venture and it's not. He'll get it in perspective eventually. Far as I'm concerned, it was a good ride. We'll call you again – maybe sooner than you think.' He said with a twinkle in his eye.

'Out of family friendship and loyalty, Tony?' She managed a wry smile. 'Not if Mr Antonello has his way – a real old-fashioned MCP. Who is he, anyway? I've never seen him before.'

'Just back from Rome where I gather he's been adding to Poppa's multi-million dollar empire. Ever heard of Antonello Fashions?'

'Who hasn't? Fabulous clothes, way beyond my pocket.'

'And that's not all. They're into merchant banking and there's talk of a new cargo line. Name any money-making pie and the old man has a finger in it. Now he has Mario back from Europe, there'll be no stopping him. Mario, the up and coming genius of the business world. So you see why I had to stop you from putting your foot in it, saying more than you should?'

Corey lifted her chin to look at him directly. 'I wish I had now. I should have told Mr Spoiled Rich Boy exactly what I thought of him.'

'Yeah. Letting that Irish temper get the better of you.'

Corey gave him a glance from under her lashes. Tony knew her all too well; she had been a part of his family for most of her teenage years. 'Now you know we're not really Irish, Tony,' she said, determined to have the last word. 'Maeve and I were both born here.'

'It's in the genes.' Tony grinned, still teasing her. 'You're just like Mario – Aussies born of immigrant parents. Maybe you have more in common than you think.'

'I doubt that.' Corey gave a theatrical shudder and held out two fingers to make a cross as if warding off the devil. 'He's rude, insensitive and everything I hate most in a man.

I feel sorry for his wife.'

'He doesn't have one. She left him.'

'Now why doesn't that surprise me?'

'An arranged marriage, I believe. Unusual in this day and age. Mario doesn't talk about it and I don't ask as it's none of my business – but I gather it didn't work out.'

'Stop it, Tony. You'll have me crying into my beer.'

'That's better.' He gave her a friendly punch on the shoulder. 'Your sense of humour's coming back. Now you will be at our party this evening? You know Pat's expecting you.'

'Oh, I don't think so, Tony.' She wrinkled her nose. 'Maybe if I'd been a winner today – but I still feel as if I've let everyone down.'

'Corey, stop that. You can't beat up on yourself every time you don't win a race. I'm more than happy with the way you conducted yourself. It was only the weight that defeated you, after all – that other horse is a donkey, nowhere near Pirate's class. So no more excuses. This is to be our night of nights and you're like a daughter to us. It won't be the same if you're not there.'

'OK.' She gave him her whispered promise.

Deep in thought, she drove slowly home, for the first time unappreciative of the shiny new pink Celica she had bought to celebrate the end of her apprenticeship and the beginning of life as a senior jockey. She really didn't feel like going to that party tonight but she loved Pat who had done her best to fill the gap left by her own mother, dead for almost seven years now. Molly O'Brien who had been the picture of health, never knowing a day's illness in her life until cancer was diagnosed during a routine check-up.

Less than three months later her beloved mother was dead.

Corey still shied away from the memory of that time. She had been fourteen, still at school and her sister, Maeve, was two years older. Michael, their father, just couldn't accept that his happy-go-lucky wife, his life's companion, had been so cruelly taken from him. Maeve had done her best to keep the family together and care for them all but Michael refused to be comforted, devoting himself to his horses and pushing his girls away. It had been hardest for Corey who reminded him too much of Molly.

Had it not been for Pat Mackintosh, Molly's best friend, who absorbed the bereaved girl into her own chaotic, unruly household when Maeve went to college, Corey might have sunk into a depression like her father. But less than two years later, he fell in love with another Irish girl, sold up the farm and followed her back to Ireland. Although Maeve could understand and accept his need to leave and opt out of their lives, Corey felt betrayed. How could he forget their mother so easily, turning his back on all of them to make a new life with a younger woman? There was a lesson to be learned from this – men were fickle, indeed.

Scarcely aware of the balmy summer evening, she ignored the crowds gathering on the bayside beaches to enjoy the relief of an evening breeze coming off the sea.

'Home' to Corey in Melbourne was an apartment in an old-fashioned house overlooking the bay. She shared this with Wendy, an airline stewardess, who worked hours as odd and unsociable as her own. When she finished her apprenticeship and was no longer required to 'live in' at the stables, she answered Wendy's ad for a flatmate, thinking to broaden her horizons. She hoped that sharing with someone from a completely different environment might give her a new perspective on life. Now she wasn't so sure.

The flat was well appointed, almost luxurious,with windows overlooking the marina and the bay. It was peaceful and lovely when Wendy wasn't home. But it was very different when she was. Wendy's life was an endless impromptu party with friends arriving at all hours of the day and night. Although Corey liked her flatmate and tolerated the relentless disco beat from the stereo or even routing the occasional couple out of her bed she knew it wouldn't do. It was time to think of moving on.

When she had left for the track in the early hours of the morning, Wendy was still away on the other side of the world but the trouble was, Corey never knew exactly when she would be back.

'Hello?' she called as she let herself in. 'Anyone home?'

Silence answered her and the hot, stuffy air in the flat told her that it had been closed up all day. Good. No one around to bully her into going to Tony's bash. She would decide about that one all on her own.

After opening a couple of windows to let in a sea breeze and taking a moment to admire the view, she kicked off her shoes, poured herself a cool drink of orange juice and went to look in her wardrobe.

The dark red suit was too hot as well as too business-like for a gala occasion. And her old faithful, the little black dress, sagged on its hanger looking so tired and worn that even a trip to the cleaners wouldn't revive it. What then? A

Chinese silk pyjama suit? Too casual. Something summery? She wrinkled her nose at the bunch of crisp, summer dresses that had taken her everywhere when she lived in the country. How could she ever have dressed like Mary Poppins?

There really was only one possibility as she had known all along. The dress she had worn to her sister's wedding and which she'd never looked at since. It reminded her too much of Jon and his perfidy.

She had met him at somebody's eighteenth birthday party – she couldn't remember whose. Everyone seemed to be turning eighteen that year. He told her he was a dress designer in his last year of college and seemed so much older, more glamorous than the kids in her usual crowd. Corey, used to the clumsy attentions of stable lads and boys her own age had never had anyone pursue her with such determination. Jon was the first man to tell her he loved her; everyone else had fought shy of it but he said it all the time. He had one of those slow smiles that made her heart turn in her chest and a way of looking at her as if she were the only girl in his world.

And so she was – until she introduced him to Maeve.

After all that high-powered attention, it hurt when he stopped calling and sending cute little messages to her mobile. Too proud to call and ask what was wrong, she waited, praying to hear from him. But when two weeks and then three went by without even a word, she had to accept he was gone and for good.

But she didn't know it was Maeve he was seeing until her sister caught up with her at the track one morning,

'No, nothing like that.' Corey smiled and relaxed, shaking her head at Wendy to indicate it wasn't Mario but that she was taking the cordless phone into her bedroom to talk in private. 'Pat, I never thanked you properly for last night. It was a wonderful party. I'm so glad I didn't miss it.'

'I'm sure.' Pat giggled. 'You made a real impression on Antonello. I could hardly believe it when Mike told me he'd carried you off into the night.'

'Don't get too excited. He was only giving me a lift home.'

'That's OK, then.' It was clear that Pat had other things on her mind. 'Corey, we need to talk. Mike and I were hoping to get round to it last night but there just wasn't time.'

'Oh dear, that sounds a bit ominous. Is anything wrong.'

'Far from it. Tony wants to make a formal offer for your services. Now the new business is up and running, we're looking for a full time stable jockey. Someone reliable and willing to get to know all the horses – ride track work and generally make a home here with us. Who better than you?'

'Oh, Pat – it sounds wonderful and I'm thrilled to be asked. But—'

'I know. It's not long since you moved to the city. And if you're happy where you are and don't want to move, we'll understand. But we do need a good rider. Someone to take an interest in the daily grind as well as the glamour of race day. Tony couldn't think of anyone he'd rather have.'

Corey was silent for a moment, her mind racing. Would it really be such a sacrifice to leave Wendy and her party-loving friends? When she moved to the city, she thought it would be fun to have a flatmate without any connections to the world of racing. But Wendy's lifestyle was so different from her own.

Pat took her silence to mean she was having some doubts. 'We've sprung this on you, I know. You must have time to think it over—'

'No, no it's not that. The job would be wonderful – Tony's getting some really good horses, these days. But I can't just move back to your place, Pat, like a college kid moving back home—'

'Oh no, love, you don't understand. You'll have your own place and be quite independent. We've had the old lodge converted and modernized to make a couple of flats for the senior staff. One of them would be yours.'

'You really have thought of everything, haven't you?'

'I hope so. But you don't have to give me an answer right now. Think it over from every angle and do what's best for you, not just for us. I can't give you all the details as the deal isn't finalized but we're in the throes of negotiating a new partnership. If it comes off, our whole operation will go into overdrive; we'll be providing training and facilities for first class horses.'

'Oh, Pat, it sounds wonderful. I'm tempted to say "yes" right away—'

'Well, don't. We want you to be completely sure. Give yourself at least twenty-four hours to decide.'

'OK. And I really should talk it over with Wendy first.'

Just as Corey was ringing off, the doorbell rang. Still thinking of Pat and the offer, she tossed the phone down and ran for the door. But Wendy was there before her, looking trim in a new grey track-suit.

At first all they could see was a doorway filled by a massive bouquet of exotic scarlet lilies and hot house roses. Until it moved aside to reveal a smiling Mario, a little taken aback to see two girls when he had expected to see only one.

'For me?' Wendy teased, gathering the flowers into her arms and breathing in the scent of the roses. 'Aren't they gorgeous.'

' 'Fraid not.' Mario smiled but firmly took them back and looked past her for Corey. 'They're for—'

'Corey – of course.' Wendy gave in with a little pout and a flirtatious glance from under her lashes. 'I'm Wendy. You'd better come in.'

'How lovely, Mario, thank you.' Corey found herself blushing under the other girl's envious gaze. She had never received such an extravagant bunch of flowers: red roses, carnations and liliums. 'But it isn't even my birthday—'

'Sometimes it's nice to have flowers for no reason at all.' He said smoothly. 'Makes it more special, somehow.'

'Let me put them in water for you.' Wendy chattered on, unfazed. 'Oh and I found this cuff link under the cushions this morning.' She held it out to Mario on the palm of her hand. 'Wouldn't be yours, by any chance?'

'Matter of fact, it is.' Mario took it, looking bemused as if only now realizing he'd lost it. 'Thanks.'

'Coffee?' She offered, flashing her professional smile. 'In here or out on the terrace?'

'In here will be fine,' Corey murmured. 'Need any help?'

'No thanks.' Wendy gave Mario another smouldering glance from under her lashes. 'You stay here and entertain your guest.'

'An obliging girl.' Mario said, raising an eyebrow at Wendy's sinuous retreat. 'Reminds me of that old-fashioned South American movie star.'

'Carmen Miranda?' Corey said, unable to resist a moment of bitchiness.

'Not *that* old!' Mario laughed. 'Katy something or other, I think.'

It wasn't long before Wendy returned with the coffee which she poured with the same flourish as if she were serving passengers in first class. Corey saw she had also taken the time to reapply lipstick and mascara, making her feel at even more of a disadvantage in her old T-shirt and shorts. Glamour came so naturally to Wendy, making her a far more suitable companion for Mario than she could ever be. She gave a small sigh at this thought, not realizing it would be audible.

'Poor Corey's exhausted.' Wendy teased as she collected the empty coffee cups. 'Not used to late nights.'

'Neither am I.' Mario said, standing up and taking it as a hint to leave.

'Oh you're not going? Not yet.' Wendy pouted. This wasn't working out at all as she'd planned. 'Corey says you're just back from Rome. We should compare notes. I'm there all the time. We must have loads of people and places in common.'

'I doubt it.' Mario didn't take the bait. 'Rome is always a seething mass of tourists and when I'm there I stay with family, not in hotels. But you make a very nice cup of coffee, Wendy. Thank you for that.'

Wendy stared at him for a moment, wide-eyed and then

snatched up the tray of empty cups and headed for the kitchen, letting the door bang behind her.

'That was a bit unkind.' Corey said as soon as Wendy was out of earshot. 'She means well really and isn't as tough as she'd have you believe.'

'If you say so. You know her better than I do. But I don't like women who make themselves that obvious,' he murmured, giving her a slow smile that made her heart lurch. He had changed from the dinner suit into a light sweater over an open-necked shirt and casual trousers, but still hadn't shaved. It gave him a raffish air. 'But why are we wasting time talking about your flatmate when I came to see you?'

'And so soon after last night.'

'I know that. But I needed to be sure.'

'Of what?'

He ignored the question, leaning forward to look at her, suddenly serious. 'That you're the same girl in daylight and it wasn't just the glamour of night. I can't afford to lose you. Not again.'

'Lose me?' she stood up to put some distance between them, alarmed by this level of emotional intensity. After the conversation she'd just had with Wendy, it was the last thing she expected. It was all too much, too soon. 'Mario, we don't know each other – we've only just met.'

'Time is only relative. It doesn't mean anything when you feel this kind of affinity with someone. I was certain you felt it, too. Don't you believe in stars colliding? In love at first sight?'

'Oh, I used to – once.' She turned aside, thinking of Jon.

'But now I think real love must come slowly or it burns itself out.'

'I used to think that, too. And I believed I had all the time in the world. It turned out I was mistaken.' He too was speaking softly, looking inward as if he were talking to himself.

'And how long would you want me for, Mario? A week – a month?' she said lightly, hoping to tease him out of the intensity of his mood. 'For the novelty of dating a jockey? You'd be surprised how many offers we get.'

'Don't make fun of this, Corey – I'm serious,' he said, catching her hand and squeezing it until she almost winced. 'To be honest, I wish you weren't a jockey at all – perched on the back of some flighty beast capable of tossing you to your death. It's too damned dangerous.'

'There's an element of danger in every sport, Mario. It's necessary. It's what keeps the spectators on the edge of their seats. But, if it makes you nervous, you ought to sell your interest in Pirate and turn your back on the racing game.'

'Too late for that, I'm afraid. I'm already committed.'

'You don't have to be. You have other interests.'

'Mostly my father's. This one is all my own. And once I'm committed to something, I like to see it through.'

'So do I.' She looked at him directly. 'I belong on the back of a horse, it's my life. It's who I am and it's not going to change. Not for you or for anyone.'

'Some day you will. Some day you'll marry and give it all up.'

'But not yet.' As his grip relaxed on her hand, she pulled

it free. 'And even if I stopped riding professionally, I'd still be involved with horses. It's in the blood.'

Unable to meet his penetrating gaze, she moved away to look out of the window. Dark clouds were gathering overhead, making the sea look grey and choppy, reflecting her unsettled mood. 'I'm drawn to you – I like you, Mario – you must know that already. But I won't make any promises I know I can't keep.' She turned and faced him. 'To be honest, I'm not sure I'll ever be the person you want me to be.'

# CHAPTER THREE

Not long after that, he left. There wasn't much more to be said. And in the wake if his departure, Wendy's criticism didn't help.

'Corey, you prize idiot.' She came straight to the point, looking pained. 'After all I said. Talk about shooting yourself in the foot.'

'You were listening?'

'No, not really. You were speaking so quietly, I couldn't hear much. But I managed to get the gist of it. Corey, the man's falling in love with you? Why didn't you just pash him and worry about the details later?'

'Because I did that with Jon and it brought me nothing but heartache.'

'Oh honestly.' Wendy raised her eyes heavenwards. 'Jon isn't anything like him.'

'I know that. But Mario scared me. All too full on, too soon.'

'Half your luck.' Wendy pulled a mock gloomy face. 'This sort of thing never happens to me.'

'But there's something strange about it. Sometimes I feel he's looking at me and seeing somebody else. I'm not sure he wants the real me. He needs an old-fashioned girl to wrap up in cotton wool and keep safe in a cabinet. I can't be like that.'

'You can pretend, can't you?'

'Whatever for? Where would that get me but straight to Heartbreak Hotel?'

'You *think* too much, that's your trouble.'

'And you don't think enough. You hurtle through life without a thought for tomorrow. You don't even plan the next minute, let alone the next hour.'

'Tell me about it.' For once, Wendy looked less than her optimistic self. 'And while we're on the subject of plans, I have some bad news. Got a letter from the landlord. Seems the old chook from across the way has been complaining about all the parties and noise. He's put me under notice and we have to leave.'

'Leave? When?'

'Soon as poss, I'm afraid. Sorry an' all that. Only got the letter today but it's been here a week. I've already put in for a transfer to Sydney. They understand about night-life there. I was hoping His Nibs might gather you up and carry you off to his place.'

'Wendy, I don't want to be gathered up and carried off anywhere – I've only just met the guy.'

'Could've worked.' Wendy shrugged. 'Damsel in distress an' all that.'

'Honestly, Wendy, you're hopeless.' Corey couldn't help but laugh.

'Yes but cute with it, aren't I?' She gave a vacant smile and fluttered her eyelashes.

Corey smiled, thinking it wasn't such a tragedy, after all;

it left her free to take up the offer from Tony and Pat.

All that remained was to tell Maeve of her plans.

As always when she rang her sister at home, she took a deep breath and crossed her fingers, hoping Jon wouldn't answer the phone. This time she was in luck.

'Corey!' Her sister sounded pleased to hear from her. 'Where have you been? It's as if you've dropped off the end of the earth. When I married, I didn't expect my sister to become a stranger.'

'Time gets away on me. You know how it is.'

'Yes, I do. Busy, busy! Jon's just the same. Too busy to be any fun, these days,' she sighed. 'The honeymoon's well and truly over.'

'Is it?' Corey chewed her lip, hoping her sister wouldn't enlarge on her problems. She felt guilty enough already for not telling her the truth about Jon.

'It's just – oh, never mind.' Corey could tell her sister was forcing herself to sound bright and cheerful. 'I'd much rather talk about you. I'd have rung before but I thought you'd be sleeping in after the big race and the party last night. Pat did ask us but Jon didn't want to go. Said he'd feel out of place with all those horsy people.'

'*You* would have liked it, though.'

'Next time, maybe. Pity about poor old Ray but what a thrill for you to pick up his ride – we saw the whole thing on the tv. Brute of a horse. You did very well to come second.'

'That's what everyone said – 'cept the owner.'

'Oh and who's that? I bet he knows nothing at all about racing.'

'And you'd be right. Mario Antonello. Maybe you've heard of him?'

'I have indeed.' Maeve sounded less than pleased. 'The golden boy – old Antonello's son and heir.'

'The very same. Well, he's new to the game and doesn't know much about horses. At first he gave me an earful for losing but was charm itself when I met him again at the party. Did I tell you I wore the famous dress?'

'About time. It looks wonderful on you.'

'And still fits like a glove. Tell Jon that Mario was very impressed with it.' Corey knew that if it *was* a copy of the Antonello original, Jon would experience more than a moment's anxiety. 'We got on so well that I spent the whole evening with him – even had supper together – he loves seafood almost as much as I do. Then we danced the rest of the night away.' Recounting the evening's events seemed to bring them vividly back to mind. She realized she had been talking to her sister for several minutes now and all her conversation had been about Mario.

'Dancing? *You*? But Corey you've always had two left feet.'

'I know but somehow I found I could dance with him. Then he gave me a lift back to town in his Ferrari.'

'Corey—' Maeve sounded hesitant, troubled even. 'Look, I don't want to play the heavy, older sister—'

'Then don't.' Corey said mildly.

'Now stop it. Don't go retreating into your shell, shutting me out. I might know a bit more about this man than you do. He's a practised charmer and has to be at least twelve to fourteen years older than you are. You do know he's been married before?'

'Tony said. He told me she left him.'

'Right. And think about that – it speaks volumes. Take care, please. You're like an innocent babe in the woods trying to manage the wolf.'

'That was Red Riding Hood, wasn't it?' Corey joked, trying to lighten her sister's mood.

'Don't be flip. This is a man who could gobble you up before breakfast.'

*Just like the one you married,* Corey thought.

'Look, Jon told me this in confidence and said I wasn't to talk about it to anyone but this is an emergency. Maybe you'll like friend Mario a lot less when I tell you what the Antonellos are really about.'

'Go on, then.' Corey said, tucking her feet up on the couch and, hugging her knees and preparing to hear the worst. For the first time in her life she wished she had learned how to smoke.

'These people are corporate raiders. They make money by taking over other people's businesses. If successful, they get absorbed into the Antonello empire – if not, the company is dismantled and their assets sold off. Either way, as independent traders, they cease to exist. Right now Jon says they're trying to make him an offer he can't refuse. They've threatened to cut off his suppliers if he doesn't accept.'

'That's illegal surely? Can they do that?'

'I think so. They take care to operate within the law. But they're quite ruthless, Jon says.'

'I don't believe it.' Corey said, wondering why Jon was making these wild accusations. Maeve didn't keep her waiting long.

'And so, to stay out of the way of the Antonellos and also to make new contacts, Jon's flying to Paris next week.'

'And you're going with him, I hope?' Corey held her breath, waiting for her sister's response.

'No, not this time. As I told you – the honeymoon's over,' Maeve said yet again. 'This trip is going to be all business, Jon says. I should be bored left on my own in the pension with nothing to do.'

'Nothing to do in Paris? Get real.'

'Anyway, it's expensive enough to send one person with the dollar this low.'

'And how long does he expect to be away?'

'Long enough to arrange a small show and maybe open a small boutique.'

'Maeve, that's crazy. You'll have no money left. A boutique in Paris will cost you a fortune – even a hole in the wall. And the problem with the Antonellos – if there really is one—'

'What do you mean *if there is one*? Are you calling Jon a liar?'

*From way back*, Corey thought but she didn't say so. 'The problem won't go away. It will still be here when he gets back.'

'Yes but we'll be in a better position to fend them off with a successful season in Paris behind us. It's now or never, Jon says.'

Promising to be in touch when she had completed her move, Corey rang off. The conversation with her sister had disturbed her. Although Maeve was doing her best to sound positive, Corey knew she was very worried indeed.

59

Why did she keep saying the honeymoon was over? And what was Jon up to? Lying to justify an expensive trip to Paris? Or was Mario really a ruthless, gangster-like executive as they said? She was attracted to Mario, yes. But what did she know about him, really?

The following morning at 4 a.m. she was back at the racecourse, involved in the day to day routine that paid her bills; exercising, track work and barrier trials. She felt at ease in this familiar environment, a world that had always been part of her life. Here at the track she was just another rider. Absorbed in this physical activity, she concentrated on the job, having no time to think of Mario or her sister's problems.

Comfortably dressed in her well-worn jodhpurs, flannelette shirt, green padded waistcoat and riding boots, she felt at home again as if yesterday had never been.

Unfortunately, word had been quick to spread concerning her near miss on Pirate. In between rides she picked up a discarded paper to find herself unfairly savaged by racing journalists, whose carefully chosen words made it clear that their criticism was as much about her gender as her ability. Also Mario's comments in the mounting yard had been overheard and enlarged upon, adding fuel to the flames.

'WHAT PRICE EXPERIENCE?' one headline screamed, the writer going on to deliver a biased account of the failures of various young riders, most of them girls. But what could she say in her own defence? How were young female riders to gain the necessary experience when they didn't get the same opportunities as their male colleagues?

Tony saw her reading it and came over to pluck it out of her hands. 'Don't read that rubbish, Corey. When journalists have deadlines to meet, they make up stories to satisfy editors. They're only there to sell newspapers, after all.'

'I know but—'

'Corey, Pat did say I wasn't to rush you but I really need to know. Have you made up your mind about joining us?'

'Yes and I'd like to accept. Soon as you like.'

'Good girl.' Tony hugged her. 'No problems with the flatmate, then?'

'Far from it. She's leaving anyway – applying for a transfer to Sydney.'

Tony blinked. 'Whoa! That's a bit sudden, isn't it?'

'It's a long story. Let's say her lifestyle caught up with her. But it leaves me free to join you with no regrets.'

'Here.' Tony took out his mobile and punched the key to ring home. 'Talk to Pat. She'll be delighted. And, when you're through, I've a filly I'd like you to look at. Entered for the Sandystone Cup on Saturday. I'd like you to ride her at track work and see if you think she's fit enough. If she is, you've got the ride. She's lightly raced and will probably start at good odds. Those joumos will have to eat their words when you bring her in as a long shot.'

Corey had surprisingly little to bring from the flat she had shared with Wendy. Her personal belongings piled easily into the trunk and the back seat of her car. It wouldn't even be necessary to make two trips. She loved her new apartment and, best of all, she had not lost her view of the sea. Certainly, a different sea. Instead of the calm of the marina,

61

there was a view of a surf beach, the open ocean pounding in on a golden, sandy beach with ti-tree on one side and windswept dunes on the other. The apartment itself was small but well-appointed with numerous built-in robes and a queen-sized bed, a convenient galley kitchen and a fully modernized bathroom containing a shower with a small tub if she wanted the luxury of a bath. It would be heaven to have a bathroom of her own without someone rattling the door handle to remind her that she was taking too long.

All this luxury and no rent to pay because it came with the job. With her few belongings around her, she felt immediately at home, Wendy and her friends becoming a distant memory.

Not for the first time, she wondered how Tony and Pat could afford such a huge step upward in lifestyle. Their former home had been pleasant enough but even after selling it at a profit, more capital would have been needed to renovate the mansion and the lodge, let alone the costs involved in bringing the stable block up to scratch and fencing a private course for training their horses. In the end she decided it wasn't her business. She was employed to ride track work and bring in the winners, helping to make the Mackintoshes's investment secure.

While searching for something else in her handbag she turned up Mario's card – not a business card but a simple one with his private mobile number.

'Call me when you're ready,' he had said on leaving, pressing it into her hand. He had made no attempt to kiss her that time.

Caught up in her hasty move from Melbourne, she

hadn't yet called him and now felt a pang of guilt. But perhaps it was for the best that fate had intervened. She would call in a week or so and casually mention that she had moved.

On the morning of the Sandystone Cup, she was up at dawn. After a quick hot shower to wake herself up, she joined Tony and Mike who were loading the horses into the trailer with some of the boys. An early start was necessary. Sandystone was almost two hundred kilometres from Melbourne and not all of the journey was on good roads.

'No Josie today?' she murmured, peering into the float.

'Not she.' Tony laughed. 'Isn't much good at getting up early, is she, Mike?'

Mike shrugged, aware that his parents scarcely tolerated his ill-tempered girl friend.

With the horses and grooms safely aboard Mike took his place at the wheel of the trailer, leaving Tony and Corey to follow in the car. Pat joined them at the last minute, already dressed in her race day finery except for an enormous hat with bright pink feathers which she placed in the back window so that it wouldn't get squashed.

The roads were quiet and the journey uneventful. No one felt like talking so Corey took the opportunity to close her eyes and nap.

Sandystone was only a small country town, off the beaten track, but it did have a good course and an original Victorian stand built by one of the wealthy pioneers for the entertainment of the locals as well as his own guests. It was a pretty little course with a heritage listing.

Shortly after 6 a.m. they were following the float down the main street of Sandystone. Like many small country towns in Victoria, it boasted a main street wide enough to allow a central nature strip with angle parking on either side. It was a gracious street, lined with mature European trees and, near the town hall, a statue of a plump, elderly Queen Victoria.

While Corey didn't care to eat much before she raced, other than the fresh fruit and muesli she had for breakfast, she accepted a bottle of water when they stopped at a service station on the way to the track.

Having checked that Sequins, the filly that she was to ride in the cup, had travelled well and was fit to run, Corey left the boys to see to the horses while she went to look for a locker in the girls' changing room. She was first to arrive but two other girls from New South Wales were also booked. Although she got on well with most of the female jockeys, there was also a friendly rivalry that existed between them.

As it was early enough, she walked around the track, both to test the going in this dry weather and also familiarize herself with the rises and turns. So far she had only one ride for the day, but there was always a chance that she might pick up another if some other jockey fell out. She would be on standby all day.

By mid-morning people had begun arriving at the course and a crowd soon started to build. For the country people who lived in this area, Cup Day was a major annual event. An Irish band set up near the mounting yard and began playing whilst half a dozen girls in short tartan skirts and clogs performed a ragged Irish jig. Riverdance had much to answer for.

Fortunately for Corey, she picked up a ride in an early race when the jockey failed to arrive after getting stuck in the traffic clogging the narrow road to the course. It wasn't the most responsive of thoroughbreds but, to the delight of its trainer, she managed to secure third place.

'Well done, lass!' he said, giving her a clap on the back that almost knocked her off her feet. 'You surprised us all. Last time I raced that lazy old nag, he came last.'

On the way back to scale, Corey's heart felt as if it turned in her chest. Out of the corner of her eye, she thought she saw an all too familiar figure – a tall man in a dark blue suit. Unmistakably from the city, he stood out against the crowd of locals in their shirt sleeves, wearing well-worn Stetsons and Akubras. Could it be Mario? Here? Surely not. But when she peered into the crowd, trying to catch a glimpse of him again, he had disappeared. She shook her head to clear it. Her guilty conscience must be playing tricks.

Back in the dressing room, she discovered that someone else had arrived – Ally Smithson, a leather-skinned, sharp-featured woman who had been a senior rider for about five years. Although her expression didn't invite conversation, Corey made a few friendly overtures in the hope of getting some news from another state. But Ally answered all questions in monosyllables, remaining aloof and unwilling to talk. All Corey learned was that she too was here to ride in the Sandystone Cup on the favoured Hot Toast.

So she turned her back on her surly companion and changed into Tony's bright pink and white colours before going out to meet Sequins' owners and receive her last minute instructions. There, another surprise awaited her. Only Pat and Tony were there – Pat, now wearing the enormous hat, the feathers echoing Tony's racing colours.

'Yes,' she answered Corey's questioning gaze. 'Sequins is mine. She didn't cost all that much but Tony had one of his hunches about her. This is the big test to see if we're right.'

Mike, who had acted as strapper, brought Sequins alongside for Corey to mount. A small, dark filly, she danced around them, skittish and nervous, upset by the boisterousness of the crowd.

'She'll settle down when you get her out there on her own,' Tony assured her. 'Needs a firm hand – likes to know who's in charge. She doesn't care to follow other horses, so you might as well take her to the front and let her lead, making them work to catch her. Hopefully, with her light weight, nobody will.'

Corey nodded, feeling the pressure of the whole family's hopes riding on her shoulders. She would do her best but much would depend on the filly's attitude when they got to the barrier stalls. If she was to lead all the way, she would have to save all her energy for the race. Luckily, Sequins settled as soon as she felt a rider in the saddle and seemed happier still as Corey rode her away from the noise of the crowd.

On her way to the barriers, Ally Smithson caught up with her – this time with something to say.

'Don't strain yourself on that little pony, will you,

O'Brien?' she said out of the corner of her mouth, surprising Corey with her venomous tone. 'I wouldn't have travelled all night to get here if I didn't think I was going to win.'

'We'll see about that.' Corey muttered, half to herself 'I don't expect to go home empty-handed, either.'

The race was over 1600 metres and the field relatively small, so Corey was able to urge Sequins to take up the running without much difficulty. The little horse responded, keeping her lead with an easy stride. It was only at the turn that Corey felt the pressure of the wall of horses behind her, ready to force her onto the fence and take over the lead. A quick glance over her shoulder told her that, if she made her move quickly, she could gain better ground in the middle of the track. Sequins responded at once, increasing her lead. The winning post was in sight but now she sensed that someone was gaining on her. A grim-faced Ally Smithson was right beside her, wielding the whip and screaming encouragement to her mount.

In the final few yards, it seemed as if Hot Toast would overtake her but Sequins found a bit more gas in the tank. She veered towards the big horse as if heading him off and Corey had to lose precious seconds correcting the filly's momentum, breaking her stride to avoid causing interference. But Sequins responded yet again, catching up with Hot Toast and they went to the line together. It wasn't long before the photo confirmed that Sequins had won by a short head, defeating the favourite. She allowed herself a small flourish of the whip as soon as the number was semaphored. It was only a country cup, but it was the biggest win so far of her career.

Ally Smithson was furious.

'You wait till I see the video,' she raved at Corey. 'You've got no chance. I'll get you suspended. You cost me the race.'

Wisely, Corey said nothing as she returned to a jubilant Tony and Pat.

'Well, done!' Pat grabbed Corey and hugged her. Then, remembering that no-one was supposed to touch the jockeys until they weighed in, she released her and took a step back, her face lit with a broad smile.

'Don't get too excited until it's "correct weight",' she warned them, nodding towards Ally who was facing grim-faced connections. 'Smithson's getting ready to lodge a protest.'

'Let her.' Tony blew out his cheeks in disgust. 'She won't get anywhere with that, the horses never touched each other.'

It was a formality, but they still endured ten anxious minutes waiting for the stewards to assess the protest before it was dismissed. Immediately after, the connections of the winning horse were asked to assemble in the mounting yard for the presentations.

'I don't have to say anything, do I?' Corey asked nervously. 'Honestly, I'd rather not.'

'You certainly do.' Pat linked her arm firmly in hers, drawing her towards the table that had been set up to present the cup. 'This is your first big win and I'm sure it's the first of many, so you'd better get used to it. Relax and enjoy yourself.'

'Congratulations, Corey.'

Already on edge at the prospect of speaking in public, Corey felt her heart lurch. She had not been mistaken earlier; it was indeed Mario she had seen. She looked up to find him watching her intently, unsmiling. For once he seemed wary, less than assured.

'Hi,' she said softly. 'I didn't expect to see you here today.'

'Well, you'd better get used to seeing him around a lot more.' Tony put an arm round her shoulders and hugged her. 'Because we're a team now. As of today, Mario joins us as a full partner in our new enterprise—'

'But Tony,' she whispered, 'why didn't you mention any of this before?'

'Because it would have been bad luck to talk about it before it was all signed and sealed. But seeing how well you and Mario get on together, we didn't think you'd mind.'

'No. No, of course not,' Corey muttered, remembering her sister's words. Mario was still watching her intently, trying to gauge her reaction to this news. Could she ignore Maeve's warning and trust her own instincts, believing him to be honest and sincere in his business dealings? Or was that being naïve? What if he really was the corporate raider Jon had described? What if he wanted more than a partnership here? What if he was getting ready to seize and take over the Mackintoshes's new enterprise?

There was only one way to find out. For reasons she had yet to find out, he had feelings for her. And the way her own heart betrayed her, leaping in her chest and making her hot and breathless just at the sound of his voice, she was equally fascinated and intrigued by him. Would it be such a hardship to spend more time with him? To play Mata Hari and find out what Mario Antonello was really about?

As she left the winners' circle and went off to change, her mind was in a turmoil.

It had just been too perfect, everything falling into place so easily. The offer from Tony and Pat which had come at exactly the right time. A secure job with a wonderful apartment thrown in, the career ahead that she'd always wanted. Even Wendy's convenient and painless departure. So why couldn't she take it all at face value and be happy? Especially after winning a country cup? Why did she feel so jittery, so insecure?

She didn't have to look far for the answer. Because of Mario, of course. Mario who made her heart sing just at the sight of him standing there in his pristine white shirt, one finger hooked into the dark blue jacket slung over his shoulder, the matching trousers close fitting over his slender hips. Mario who knew very little about the racing industry but who would now have a say in her working life. Mario, who disapproved of women in racing. Mario, who was so wrong for her and with whom she was probably falling in love.

There! Now she had admitted that possibility, if only to herself, it would be easier to deal with wouldn't it? Or not. In the changing rooms, she was relieved to find no sign of Ally Smithson – she had enough to think about without facing another confrontation with that one. She showered carefully this time, taking the time to wash her hair and dressed quickly in her everyday clothes and boots, wishing she had bothered to bring some make-up. Never mind. Maybe she wouldn't have to face him just yet and would have the time to find out the true level of his involvement and talk it over with Tony on the way home.

But when she left the changing rooms, only Mario was there waiting for her a slow smile spreading over his face as he saw her.

'What is it? What?' she snapped, nerves making her irritable.

'It's you. You look like a schoolgirl without any make-up.'

'Oh? So you have a thing for schoolgirls, do you?' She was determined not to take it as a compliment.

'What have I done now?' His smile faded. 'I'm only here to offer you a lift.'

'But Tony and Pat—?' she said, looking round for them.

'Pat took off for home straight away. It won't be a late night as everyone will be tired but she wants to organize a dinner to celebrate. I offered to wait for you, that's all. But if that doesn't suit you, I'm sure Tony can find room for you in the float . . .'

'No, no,' she said quickly, thinking of the comfort of the Ferrari up against being jolted and rattled along dirt roads in the float. 'I was surprised, that's all. Didn't mean to sound ungrateful.'

'That's OK, then. No offence taken, if none meant.' He grabbed her saddle and bag, leading the way to the car.

71

# CHAPTER FOUR

COREY didn't realize how tired she was until she buckled herself into that comfortable seat and breathed in the now familiar smell of expensive leather, combined with the subtle tang of his aftershave. For a moment she was transported back to the night they met, that magical night of the party, the memory of his kisses overwhelming her, making her heart step up its beat.

Mentally, she gave her head a shake. She really would have to get over these feelings. After all, *a kiss is just a kiss* as the song goes. She'd be a fool to read too much into it. Surely, it would have meant no more to him than kissing a stranger at midnight on New Year's Eve – a way to bring a pleasant evening to a close.

To drag herself back to reality, she remembered Wendy's advice concerning rich boyfriends. *It won't last. Just make the most of it and grab all the presents while you can.* Now that might be OK for Wendy but Corey wasn't made that way. She couldn't bring herself to be so mercenary or start a relationship unless her feelings were involved. She understood

that these days most people didn't take intimacy half as seriously as she did – her experiences with Jon had taught her
that much – but she still didn't find it easy to accept. Would
Mario be like that, as well? Expecting her to be 'grown up'
about it, taking casual sex as a matter of course? A pleasure
to be enjoyed and just as quickly forgotten? She had been
raised differently, always taught that intimacy should take
place only within a committed relationship; she shouldn't
give herself without believing she was loved in return.

And now that Mario was in business with Tony, that put
a whole new complexion on everything – they could be
thrown together almost daily. Would familiarity breed
contempt? And he must have other girl friends. How would
she feel when he invited them to visit the complex and she
had to watch him paying attention to somebody else? She
closed her eyes, wincing at the very thought of it. *Stupid,
Corey, stupid!* She mocked herself. *You've talked yourself in
and out of this before anything's happened. Snap out of it!*

'You're a strange one,' he said, breaking in on her reverie
as he drove through the town on the way back to the main
road. 'Your first really big win – a country cup, no less –
and you're sitting there looking as if you have the weight of
the world on your shoulders. You should be jumping up
and down and shouting for joy.'

'Inside, I am.' She glanced at him, biting her lips. 'I don't
make a fuss about it, that's all.'

'Hmm,' he said, giving her a quick glance before returning his attention to the road. 'I don't think so. I sense
something more. It's the partnership, isn't it? I watched
your face as Tony was telling you and you looked more

73

shocked than surprised. Is it so terrible, then? The idea of working with me?' He didn't look at her this time, keeping his gaze on the road. 'Come on, Corey, don't hold back. I want to know how you feel. Be honest with me.'

For a moment she paused, considering a bland cliché for an answer and decided against it. He was demanding honesty and deserved nothing less than the truth. If it caused a rift between them that couldn't be helped. Better now rather than later when her feelings had become too deeply involved. So she took a deep breath and waded in.

'Mario, your views on women in racing are hardly a secret. It's all right for us to be strappers, to muck out the stables and even ride track work if there aren't enough boys for the job. Other than that, we can turn up dressed in our best to decorate the stands. But as for competing with men as professional riders – no. That's strictly a male preserve.'

He seemed taken aback. 'Do I really come across as old-fashioned as that?'

'I'm afraid so.' She found herself smiling. 'But you said it, Mario. I didn't.'

'It's nothing personal, Corey. Well, that's not strictly true. It's because – because—' He glanced at her eager face and the words stuck in his throat. Even after all this time, he found it hard to talk about Rina. 'Let's just say it isn't as simple as that.'

'No!' Corey felt a flash of irritation. She had done her best to answer him honestly and she didn't think it was fair for him to clam up. 'That's a cop out if ever I heard one. I was straight with you – why can't you be straight with me?'

'I can't tell you,' he muttered. 'Not yet. This isn't the time.'

74

'Great,' she said, sitting back and folding her arms. 'Thanks a lot, Mr Mysterious.'

'Yes but I'm not the only one being secretive and mysterious.' He was quick to take up her mood. 'Why didn't you tell me you were leaving town? I thought we were friends.'

'Very new friends. Some people would say we were scarcely acquainted.'

He hit the steering wheel with the heel of his hand. 'I'm not talking of *some people* – I'm talking about us. You promised to ring me, to keep in touch – so why didn't you?'

'I don't know – it all happened so quickly. Wendy was under notice and we had to get out. Luckily it coincided with the offer from Tony and Pat.'

'So when did you mean to tell me? Next week maybe? Next year?' He bit the words out, his voiced clipped with anger, hands gripping the wheel. Still he kept his eyes on the road, not looking at her. She glanced at his profile, beginning to be scared. She hadn't seen this side of him since she lost the race on Pirate.

'If you'd wanted to, you could have found me through Tony and Pat.'

'Yeah? And how would that sound? *By the way, what happened to that jockey of yours? I want to take her out.*'

Partly from nerves and partly because she was so delighted to hear him say it aloud, Corey giggled. This irritated him further.

'Dammit woman, I won't be laughed at. Can't you take anything seriously?'

He slammed his foot to the floor and the Ferrari took off like a bird in flight, the wheels complaining and sliding on the dirt road, the trees on either side flipping by so fast they appeared to be spinning.

'Mario, slow down!' she said, clinging to the seat in panic. 'You're going too fast.'

'Really?' He glanced at her, a wild look in his eye. 'I thought you liked speed? I thought you liked living dangerously?'

'Only when I'm in control of it.'

Wrong answer. The car slewed as he pressed his foot to the floor to go faster than ever. She was genuinely frightened now. In these brief moments of twilight, with visibility poor, it was more dangerous than ever for him to be speeding. She made one last desperate attempt to make him stop.

'Mario, please stop this! You're scaring me.'

He heard her at last and took a deep breath, easing the screaming engine to a more normal speed, shaking one hand then the other to break the tension. She too let go a long breath, only now realizing she had been holding it. He slowed right down, pulled the car off the road under a stand of trees and turned off the motor. The silence after the roar of that powerful engine, seemed more complete than ever.

Still furious at his reckless behaviour, Corey opened the door and climbed out, meaning to walk away from both Mario and his car. But her legs were still shaking and would hardly support her. So she closed the door and leaned back against it instead. She heard rather than saw him get out and walk around to confront her, closing her eyes to avoid that searching gaze.

'I lost my temper,' he said, offering an explanation rather than an apology. 'I can't stand people laughing at me when I

want to be serious. Anna used to do it all the time and I—'
He paused, shaking his head once again as if he couldn't say
more.

'Anna?' she prompted, opening her eyes.

'My wife – ex-wife, that is,' he corrected quickly. 'We
married to please our parents. It was a big mistake.'

'There you are, you see,' she said softly, turning away. 'I
know so little about you.'

'And if you keep avoiding me, how are you going to
learn more?' He spoke softly, placing his hands gently,
almost tentatively on her shoulders and turning her to face
him as if he expected her to take fright and pull away. 'You
can trust me, Corey. I won't hurt you. I never play games.'

And as she looked into his cool blue eyes and knew the
intensity of his feeling, she relaxed in his gasp. His face
loomed closer and she knew he was going to kiss her. Still
it wasn't too late to haul back. A sensible girl would stand
on her dignity and say he had read the signals all wrong,
that he was mistaken in her. But after all that had
happened, Corey didn't feel like being sensible, not now,
not today. If she were to pay for it later in heartache, so be
it. That didn't concern her now.

She welcomed him into her arms and parted her lips to
match his kiss, giving in to the inevitable. She was still
shivering but with excitement and sexual tension rather
than fright. And when he pinned her against the car,
moving his knee to part her legs, allowing her to feel the
full length of his strong body against her own, she didn't
resist. It amazed her to discover that he was tense as she
was, his heart pounding just as urgently as her own.

He smelled wonderful, his cologne mingling with the sharp tang of fresh sweat, the atmosphere still crackling with the electricity of his temper, only just under control. Holding nothing back now, she let him deepen the kiss, matching his demands with her own and burying her fingers in his thick hair, drawing him closer to make his mouth more accessible to her own. She had never felt like this, not even with Jon and the hunger Mario aroused in her caught her completely off guard.

He stood this refined torture for as long as he could until he had to break the kiss at last, catching her hands as they stared into each other's faces, both breathing heavily, equally surprised by the ferocity of their need. He was first to recover and break the mood, calling them back from those dizzying heights that had almost overwhelmed them.

'I don't think you know the strength of those little hands, Corey O'Brien.' Gently, he unfastened her fingers, releasing her grip.

Laughter quickly dissolved the tension and he kissed her again, this time with more tenderness than urgency. Deftly, he unfastened several buttons of her shirt, watching her face to gauge her reaction before moving his hand inside to caress her breast with the tips of his fingers, making her sigh with pleasure. Clearly he was a man of many moods. This time, when they came up for air, he glanced at his watch and sighed. 'We should get going,' he said. 'We'll be late for Pat's dinner.'

'I doubt it,' she said, trying to match his humour although her voice was still shaky. 'You must have covered all of fifty kilometres in five minutes.'

'We were perfectly safe. My uncle's a racing driver – he taught me to drive.'

'On dirt roads?'

'Yes. He taught me to make emergency stops on a skid pan.'

'I don't care. Unless you promise to slow down, I'll take my chances and hitch a ride home instead.'

'Will you, indeed?' He gave a bark of laughter. 'Who with? A bunch of redneck farmers who might drag you into the bushes to have their wicked way with you?'

'You have such a lurid imagination.' She smiled ruefully, shaking her head.

'Not really. I was just thinking what I'd like to do if I found you wandering out here alone on the road.' He opened the car door and subjected her to a wolfish grin as he ushered her inside.

'Now that really inspires me with confidence,' she teased, keeping it light although her heart was still pounding from the intensity of their recent embrace, her lips still bruised and tingling from his kisses. All the same, she reminded herself, she shouldn't read too much into it. Surely, it was no more than a casual encounter, triggered by the excitement of driving too fast. And although their worlds might touch briefly through a common interest in racing, Mario's lifestyle was so different from her own. His was a world of high fashion and glamorous women, gala events and late nights. In her own, the needs of the horses came before everything else. She rose early and was usually asleep before 10 at night. So what could he possibly see in her?

But in spite of all her attempts to be calm and nonchalant, her heart insisted on pulsating merrily, swelling with the joy of new love.

'What made you take up an interest in racing?' she asked him, voicing at least some of her thoughts. 'It seems such a far cry from fashion and—'

'Exactly,' he laughed. 'My father would like me to concentrate on the business to the exclusion of everything else – as he does. But I've always loved horses – especially thoroughbreds – so I decided to buy one.'

'Pirate? He's wonderful.'

'I know. And when Tony said he needed a partner, I jumped at the idea.'

Corey gave him a quick sideways glance, remembering Maeve's warning about the Antonellos and their business tactics. Yet Mario seemed so straightforward and honest, always ready to speak his mind. Surely, he wasn't a ruthless businessman like his father?

They arrived back at the mansion late enough to cause comment.

'We expected you to be here ages before the float,' Tony said with a glance at Pat who greeted them with pointed looks and raised eyebrows, having noted the flushed faces and slightly dishevelled clothes. 'Beginning to think you'd had an accident.'

Quickly, Corey pushed her fingers through her untidy hair as Mike and Josie nudged each other and exchanged knowing glances, pleased to see the heat was off them for a change.

'We paused for a moment to take in the view,' Corey said at last. 'Sunset was lovely tonight.'

'Yes,' Mario nodded. 'The view was especially lovely from where I was sitting.' *And still is*, he thought, smiling into Corey's eyes. Her blush deepened as she smiled back. Seeing Pat was about to make further comment, he changed the subject by proposing a toast as Tony handed him a glass of wine.

'To Antonello and Mackintosh.' He smiled around the table at all of them, raising his glass. 'May this be the first of many successful days.'

Half an hour later with Pat's nourishing ragout inside them, everyone started to yawn. Mike and Josie excused themselves, Mario said farewell to his hosts and offered to escort Corey to her door.

'Good heavens, Mario, she can't come to much harm crossing the yard,' Pat started to say, only to break off as Tony hushed her and turned off all the lights at the front of the house, plunging them all into darkness.

As their eyes adjusted to the gloom, Mario took Corey's hand as they slowly walked down the drive towards the gate house. In the adjoining flat, the lights were already out. John, Tony's stable foreman, would have to be up before everyone, preparing the horses for the day's work.

As they approached her front door, Corey's mind was racing. After the way she had behaved earlier, Mario was surely expecting to share her bed. But was she ready for this? Earlier, the urgency of his kisses had taken her totally by surprise and she was no less startled by her own response – her own lack of self control. Had they been anywhere else but roadside, she might have given herself to him there and then without further thought.

But after dinner with the Mackintoshes and seeing Pat's obvious lack of enthusiasm, she was thinking again. And it wouldn't do to appear too easy; she didn't want him to think her cheap and promiscuous, ready to sleep with any man. How could she put him off without offending or discouraging him entirely?

At her door, he surprised her by lifting her off her feet and starting to kiss her again; she sensed his excitement and could feel the suppressed passion behind it. His eyes were already darkening with that hunger she found so hard to resist.

'Open the door,' he whispered. 'Let me carry you in.'

'Oh, Mario.' She buried her face in his shoulder. 'It's late and I really—' Even to her own ears, the excuse sounded lame and half-hearted.

'Just open the door.' Although he spoke softly, it was an order, not a request as he set her down on her feet again. 'I'm not a brute, Corey. I won't do anything you don't want.'

*But that's just it,* she thought. *It is what I want.* All the same she opened the door and then turned to face him. 'I really don't think this is a good idea—'

'Because of Pat?' He was quick to divine the reason for her sudden change of heart. Pat didn't know how to be subtle and her disapproval was obvious. All the same, he wasn't about to let an over-protective hen separate him from his quarry – not now he was this close. Let Corey escape him now and he might never get her back. It wasn't as if she didn't want him – he knew she did – and that there could be something special between them if she would only relax and let him in.

82

'Coffee, Mario,' she said briskly. 'I'll make you coffee and then you really will have to go home.'

'Just like old times,' he murmured, following her into the flat, taking in the simple decor. Corey had only the furniture Pat had provided; apart from a few family photographs, she hadn't had time to find pictures or put up ornaments to make it more like home.

She was hoping he would sit in the lounge while she made coffee and pulled herself together but no such luck. He followed her into the kitchen, came up behind her and placed his hands on her shoulders.

'It's not coffee I want, Corey,' he said softly, leaning down so that his breath tickled her ear. 'It's you.'

She closed her eyes and relaxed against him. This was heady stuff. A far cry from Jon who had accepted her with a kind of deprecating humour, making her feel less than adequate when he criticised her boyish slenderness, her small, athlete's breasts. No. She wouldn't think about Jon or his many small cruelties; he was Maeve's problem now.

Turning to face Mario, she made no complaint when he lifted her off her feet, this time to carry her to her bed. He kicked open the bedroom door, which wasn't properly closed, dropped her on the bed and removed her boots, flinging them away across the room. He kicked off his own shoes and lay down beside her, stopping all thought of objection with his kisses. His stubble rasped her chin but it felt wonderful just the same. Feeling rather than seeing, she unbuttoned his shirt, thrilled by the smoothness of his skin and the tautness of the muscles beneath. Surprisingly, for all that he was so dark haired, he had no hair on his chest although he did have soft hair on his forearms. Gradually, she became aware that he was undressing her, too, and she opened her eyes to watch him doing it; first her shirt and then the bra until she was naked to the waist. He had beautiful hands, strong and brown, with square-tipped, sensitive fingers and she shivered with delight as he played with her breasts, teasing the nipples until they were erect. She brought his head down to them, encouraging him to take them into his mouth. She could feel his hardness pressing against the restraint of their clothes and they broke free for a moment to tear off their trousers, before falling into each other's arms yet again.

It felt so right and she wanted him so much it was a growing ache inside her. He too groaned as she touched the silken tip of his member which moved involuntarily in her hand.

'Do you have something?' she murmured, wondering what she would do if he didn't. It had been so long since she had considered sex, he had caught her totally unprepared. He left her briefly to take a condom out of his jacket pocket and allowed her to fit it over his aroused member.

'Ready now?' He kissed her deeply again before easing her on to her back and plunging inside.

Not having had sex for so long, she cried out at first with the shock of it but he stopped her mouth with another long kiss as he moved gently at first and then more purposefully inside her. Holding her and still caressing and teasing her breasts, he watched until she was ready to reach her climax so that he could come with her.

Afterwards, he didn't withdraw at once but stayed inside her as she gradually returned to earth from what had felt like a journey to the stars. When it really was over at last, he moved away gently and gave her a long, slow smile. He didn't have to ask if it had been good for her; her breathlessness and the brightness of her eyes told him everything.

'I will kiss you all over,' he told her – and he did – his tongue probing corners of her body she didn't even know could be sensitive to his touch.

'I know so little,' she confessed. 'You'll have to show me what you like.'

'Just hold me.' His voice was a passionate growl as he drew her hands down to touch him until he was ready to make love yet again. This time it was more leisurely, less frantic but, if anything, the pleasure was more exquisite than before as they learned to be less greedy, more at ease with one another. At last, although it was well after midnight, lying in each others arms, they slept.

When Corey's alarm went off at 5 a.m. she turned over, expecting to find Mario still lying beside her but there was only empty space in the bed. Some time, during the early hours, he had silently dressed and left. Feeling bereft and blinking with weariness, she turned off the alarm and sat up, wishing it wasn't her habit to sleep so heavily; she would have liked him to wake her to say good-bye.

She hauled herself out of bed and stood up to examine herself in the mirror, looking for evidence that she hadn't dreamed the whole thing. Her face and chin still glowed from the contact with his stubble, her nipples and breasts, having been neglected for so long, were pink and a little sore from his passionate attentions. Carried away by the moment, she had forgotten totally about the need for protection. Fortunately, he had been prepared. Was he always prepared, she wondered, keeping condoms in the pocket of his jacket? The more she thought about it, the more her happy mood evaporated as the doubts began to creep in. What if he were a playboy as Wendy suggested? A man whose passions were quickly sated? In his own way he could be just as dangerous as Jon – a man who could make a woman believe that he loved her – but for only one night. She could have sworn that he had been there with her every inch of that way; that his involvement had been as intense, as passionate as her own. But was that just because she wanted it to be so? Were her instincts to be trusted or had she been deceived yet again?

She almost ran to the shower to wash all contact with him from her body and when she was done, there was no lingering smell of his cologne to tantalize her, only her own lavender soap and talc. There! Now she felt more like her own woman again. She wasn't the first girl to be seduced into spending a night with a man and certainly wouldn't be the last. But she was feeling the loss, hurting already. He had made her feel so desirable – beautiful even – that the thought of losing him, never holding him close to her ever again was too much to bear. Even as she dressed herself quickly for work and dragged on her boots, she found herself unable to see through the tears that suddenly blinded her. Impatiently, she brushed them away.

As Mario drove away from the mansion, slowly and quietly, so as not to wake the sleeping household, he too had a lot on his mind. What had possessed him to be so thoughtless, so greedy? Downright selfish enough to put his own lusts, his own desperate needs, in front of her own? How could he take such cruel advantage of an inno-cent girl? Not quite innocent, thank God, she had not been a virgin. At least he didn't have that on his conscience.

He knew he would never stop loving Rina – his disas-trous marriage to Anna had shown him as much. But Corey was brave and honest and with so much to offer the right man – for just a moment he had forgotten he wasn't. She deserved more, so much more than to be second best, a substitute for his lost love.

He glanced at himself in the rear view mirror, seeing nothing but guilt in his eyes. In the throes of their passion, he had almost cried out, calling her Rina. Fortunately, he had stopped himself just in time.

And what would Corey expect of him now? Certainly not to be dumped or ignored like a one-night stand. And after the way he had acted last night, she must think they were all but engaged. Going over it all again, he realized he had spoken no words of commitment, not even of love. Although passion had overtaken them – no doubt of that – it had been expressed only physically.

Then he had gone from her, leaving no message, not even a promise to call again, giving her every right to be angry and disappointed. Maybe he should leave it at that, being cruel to be kind. But there was a part of him didn't want to leave it at all – the selfish Mario who wanted her to lie in his arms, watching her eyes go stormy with passion for him yet again. He closed his eyes briefly to banish the thought. No good dwelling on what could never be.

In his line of work he met many beautiful women. Girls like Wendy who wanted no more than a good time and who drifted in and out of his life as pleasant interludes and with no commitment on either side. But Corey wasn't like those girls. Not mica but pure gold. A woman who gave; without restraint, an intuitive, instinctive lover who responded to his touch as a fine musical instrument will respond to the hands of a maestro.

He glared at himself once more in the mirror. It would do him no good to remember that now. It was over; it had to be. The next time she looked at him it would be with ice in those fine, grey eyes. That thought didn't make him happy.

He sighed and put on some gloomy classical music to suit his mood as the car sped along the motorway on its way to the city. He didn't trouble to access his answering machine; he knew it would be full of messages, clamouring for his attention. It would be a while before he could indulge himself to think of Corey O'Brien again.

Fortunately for Corey, Tony was so busy with horses needing exercise that morning that he didn't see her wan expression and tear-stained eyes. She wasn't so lucky with Pat who was quick to notice them when she came down from the house, bringing coffee and toast for their breakfast. Leaving Tony and the men to talk among themselves, she drew Corey to one side.

'Are you feeling all right, love?' She peered at her. 'You look a bit peaky today.'

'Just tired.' Corey responded with what she hoped was a bright smile.

'Hmm.' Pat wasn't to be diverted. 'I didn't sleep all that well myself and I saw Mario's car sloping off some time after four. Don't tell me you were just sitting up drinking coffee and talking till that hour. Now darling, I don't want to start sounding like a mum but—'

'Then don't,' Corey said lightly. She felt foolish enough about Mario already and the last thing she needed was a lecture from Pat. 'You don't have to worry about me. I'm old and ugly enough to look out for myself.'

'You're not old and ugly at all which is part of the problem.' Pat smiled ruefully. 'But it's your life, Corey, and I'm not going to interfere. Just remember that Mario isn't a boy – he's a man who's already been married and—'

'I do know, Pat. And you can forget it, anyway, because I doubt if it goes any further than this. I won't be spending much time with Mr Antonello from now on.'

'Mr Antonello now, is it? Oh, dear.' Pat raised her eyebrows and sighed. 'Ah well, it's probably all for the best,' she said, deciding it wasn't. She had never seen Corey looking so pinched and miserable, not even when Maeve was getting married to Jon. Truly, she thought of Corey as the daughter she'd never had and it was her dearest wish to see her with a new love; someone nearer her own age perhaps and carrying no baggage from previous relationships. Besides being too old for her, Mario Antonello was way out of her league.

Corey waited, half hoping to hear from him although that hope faded a little each day. But Mario stayed away, communicating with Tony by e-mail as week after week went by. So she threw herself into work until she was so physically exhausted, she didn't have time to think. She went to bed early and was one of the first to be downstairs in the morning, helping with the regular work of the stables.

In hindsight, she realized she had no one but herself to blame for Mario's flight. She ought to have put up more than a token resistance that night. But having been celibate for a year she had found herself needy as he was. Carried away by the moment, she had flung herself at his head with no thought for the future. If he thought her amoral and easy, it was nobody's fault but her own.

She accepted a full card for a Saturday country meeting, this time on the peninsula, closer to home. Having ridden two winners for Tony in the early races, she was feeling on top of her form and looking forward to beating her personal best until she bumped into Ally Smithson halfway through the day.

'You owe me, little Miss Sandystone Cup,' Ally glared at her. 'And I mean to win today's feature race or I'll know the reason why.'

'The best horse will win.' Corey tried to look as if she didn't care although Ally's spiteful expression made her uneasy. 'I don't throw races for anyone.'

'Did I ask you to?' Ally opened wide eyes. 'I just said you owe me, that's all.'

At the barriers, she was no happier to find she had been placed next to the woman, fortunately this time with nothing to say. The track was small and the field larger than usual, so she knew it was going to be tricky. Fortunately her mount, Sequins again, was becoming used to the routine of race day.

90

The barriers opened and they were off. This time Corey elected to stay at the back, letting the early contenders fight it out among themselves. When the field was regrouping, close to the finish, she would choose the fence, if she could see a way to slip through unexpectedly. Otherwise she would have to race Sequins around the whole field. The race wasn't long and for a moment she thought she was going to be trapped behind a wall of horses until the field drifted away from the fence, leaving her the clear run she wanted on the inside.

'Go Sequins – go now!' she called to the filly who flattened her ears and lengthened her stride, heading for home until she heard a yell behind her.

'Get out of the way, O'Brien – I'm coming through.'

Momentarily distracted, Corey forgot a cardinal rule and looked back to see if she really was hindering Smithson. It was sufficient to break Sequins' stride and make her stumble against the horse beside her, also winding up for the finish. With a scream of triumph, Ally rode through to win, waving her whip, the horse Corey had contacted taking only second place and Sequins third.

While the winning connections celebrated noisily nearby, Corey took her saddle from Sequins and went to weigh in. She considered making a fuss and reporting Smithson for causing her to make a mistake but decided against it. It was a mean trick Ally had played on her but she shouldn't have fallen for it. Correct weight was announced and she breathed a sigh of relief, believing that was the last she would hear of it. Until she received a summons to attend an enquiry in the Stewards' Room, something which had never happened before. She was relieved when Tony offered to go with her.

'Say as little as possible,' he muttered. 'And remember to show respect.'

'But Tony, it was an accident they must understand that. I didn't mean to do anything wrong.'

He glanced at her and would have had more to say except the door opened and they were ushered in.

'Well now, Miz O'Brien.' The chief steward subjected her to his disapproving gaze. 'I want you to take a look at the video of that last race. Then you can tell me what you have to say for yourself.'

Biting her lips, Corey watched the replay of the race that showed all too clearly what had happened. When she looked over her shoulder at Ally, Sequins became distracted and drifted into the horse beside her, costing them both the race.

'It was a mistake,' she whispered. 'I'm so sorry. I won't let it happen again.'

'Not good enough,' he snapped. 'You think you can say "sorry" and make everything go away.'

'Of course I don't. I've had a clean record so far. This is the first time I've been criticized for my riding of any horse.'

'And if you go on the way you're going, it won't be the last.'

'That's not fair!'

'Corey—' Tony put a hand on her shoulder to calm her. He knew that such outbursts wouldn't help her case.

'I'm not here to waste time arguing about what is or isn't

fair. There's no doubt in my mind that you could have caused a serious accident, especially in front of a large field. And I take a poor view of jockeys who lose concentration and put other horses and riders at risk.'

'I didn't lose concentration. Ally Smithson shouted at me and I was distracted.'

'Really? You can be distracted by shouts on a race course? Then you must spend half your time "being distracted", Miz O'Brien.'

Frustrated by the man's contemptuous attitude, Corey felt her temper rise. Tony also sensed this and gave her a warning glance. She took a deep breath to calm herself.

'I was going to suspend you for a month, Miz O'Brien, but in view of your attitude, I've decided to make it six weeks. You rode two winners today already. Sometimes that makes a jockey careless and over-confident. Go home now and take the six weeks to think about what I've said.'

'Yes, sir,' she said, staring at the floor. She didn't dare look up at him in case he saw the tears of fury stinging her eyes. 'Thank you, sir.'

She walked away from the stewards' office stunned. This was the first time anything like this had happened, her record having been unblemished before.

# CHAPTER FIVE

'IT doesn't matter,' Tony reassured her later. He had been surprised by the storm of weeping this minor setback produced from Corey. As a rule, she wasn't a girl who cried easily. 'These things happen and to the best of them. After all, it's only six weeks.'

'Six whole weeks,' Corey wailed.

'And it isn't as if we don't have plenty for you to do here.'

'I know, Tony. But it's so unfair. Smithson did that on purpose. She planned it.'

'She's just a jealous cow.' Tony pulled a sour face that did look amazingly like Ally. 'Because she knows she'll never be half the rider you are.'

'Oh Tony, you're wonderful.' She hugged him. 'What would I do without you?'

'Ride for somebody else, I suppose,' he said, fending her off. He wasn't the most demonstrative of people, particularly in front of his staff.

That evening, Corey received a phone call from Maeve. Guilt overwhelmed her as she recognized her sister's voice.

She had been so caught up in her own emotional problems, followed by the suspension, that she had scarcely had time to think about Maeve.

'Corey, I need a favour – rather a big one, I'm afraid.' Maeve sounded close to tears.

'You sound terrible.' Corey said without thinking. 'Are you OK?'

'Not really – no—' Maeve said, losing the battle with her tears. It was nearly a minute before she could speak coherently.

'Maeve, tell me what's happened? What's wrong?' Corey's heart plummeted; she knew it must have to have something to do with Jon. Her sister didn't take long to confirm it.

'It's Jon. He's been in France for months and won't tell me when he's coming back. He says his new line has been a great success over there but the bills are mounting up here and he won't send me any money to pay them.'

'You want me to lend you some money to tide you over? That's easy—'

'No, Corey. I need you to lend me enough to get to Paris and see what he's up to.'

'Oh, Maeve, is that wise? I'll lend you the money, of course. I've had a few good wins lately – but—'

'Don't give me a lecture, please. I know that for some reason – whatever – you don't like Jon. But I'll go crazy if I don't see him.'

'OK,' Corey said slowly. 'Is it all right if I send you a cheque or will I come into town—'

'Can you come into town? Tomorrow? I need to pay cash

95

for my ticket. If you give me a cheque the bank's going to keep it.'

'Maeve, just how much financial trouble do you have?'

'I don't know.' She sounded once more on the verge of tears. 'We wouldn't be in financial trouble at all if it weren't for the Antonellos.'

At the mention of that name, Corey's heart lurched. 'Oh?'

'That evil old man has cut off all Jon's lines of credit. He's told all our suppliers to ask for their money up front – before it became a bad debt.'

'But why should he do that, Maeve? What does he possibly have to gain?'

'I don't know. I guess it's just another way of forcing us to sell out to him.'

'I still find that hard to believe. The Antonellos are big business, Maeve. They have no reason to stoop to anything as vindictive as that.'

'Are you sure?'

Corey fell silent for a moment, thinking about it. At present, her own feelings about Mario were nothing if not mixed. Both Tony and Pat thought highly of him and trusted him implicitly, allowing him to share their dream. Could she really imagine him trying to sabotage Jon's business?

'Corey? Corey, are you still there?'

'Yeah. Look, I'll see you tomorrow. We'll talk it all over then.'

She put the phone down and frowned. She didn't like this at all. Her sister needed much more than a one-way ticket to Paris and she wasn't about to let her leave without the means to return. She couldn't go empty-handed either; she would need pocket money while she was away.

It had been a while since she had seen her sister and she was shocked to see her so down. Maeve's usually shiny blonde hair was dull and looked as if it hadn't been washed for a week. She had lost so much weight, her clothes hung from her shoulders and there was a sore on her lip that looked as if it had been there for some time. It was clear that she hadn't been eating properly for weeks. At first Corey didn't say anything but hugged her sister as she wept hot tears into her neck.

'Thank you for coming so quickly, Corey. It's so good to see you.'

'You should have called me before.'

'I – I – oh, Corey.' Maeve's face contorted again.

'It's OK, darling, I'm here now.' Corey held her sister and let her cry again, remembering that when they were young, it had always been the other way round. Maeve had always been the one to comfort *her*. It brought tears to her own eyes to see her sister, the beauty of the family, brought so low. 'First things first. You're getting a decent meal and then we're off to the hairdresser and a good make-up counter. If you really are going to Paris—'

'I am. And please don't try to talk me out of it.'

'I wasn't going to. But Paris is one of the smartest cities in the world, so you'll have to look the part.'

'Corey, you're wonderful. I'm beginning to feel better already.'

With Maeve looking more like her old self again, they went to the bank and the travel agent. A cancellation meant she could fly to Sydney and from there directly to Paris the very next day.

'I won't need a return,' Maeve said when the girl at the agency asked about it. 'I'll come back with Jon – he'll buy me a ticket, then.'

'You're having an open return,' Corey insisted. 'And if you've any sense, you won't even tell Jon you've got it.'

'Why not?' For the first time Maeve turned on her sister. 'What has he ever done that you shouldn't trust him?'

Corey shook her head and spoke to the travel agent, unwilling to get into that argument here. 'And she'll need a thousand dollars in travellers' cheques.'

'Honestly, Corey, I won't. I feel bad enough letting you pay for the ticket.'

'Take it, anyway. At least then you'll have some independence if—' She faltered, biting her lip.

'If what?'

'If things don't work out as you think.'

'For heaven's sake, Jon is my husband. You act as if he's not going to be pleased to see me.'

Corey couldn't say more in front of the travel agent but in the end Maeve accepted the thousand dollars. Even so, it seemed a pitifully small amount to take to an expensive city like Paris. But Maeve, now she had her plane ticket safe in her handbag, had risen from her depression to become determinedly optimistic.

Back at the flat, Corey telephoned Pat to explain that she would stay the night with her sister and return after taking her to the airport in the early hours of the morning. She spent most of the evening fielding phone calls from Jon's many creditors while Maeve sat hugging her knees and biting her lips, too timid to speak to them.

Inevitably, so many unanswered questions led to a tension between them but Corey knew better than to press her sister while she was in this mood.

Used to getting up early, Corey responded immediately to their alarm call at 4.30 a.m. unlike Maeve who grumbled and groaned, unable to wake up until she was pushed into the shower. Fortunately, her bag had been packed the night before.

Quantas International was busy, even at that hour, and they had to queue for Maeve's boarding pass. At the moment of parting, Maeve turned to her sister and hugged her, eyes once more brimming with tears.

'I'll always be grateful,' she whispered. 'I couldn't have done this without you.'

'Hope it works out,' Corey said, knowing how lame that sounded. Somehow she couldn't bring herself to say *Love to Jon*. She was all too aware that she herself could have been standing there in Maeve's shoes – a wife neglected – if not deserted – chasing an errant husband halfway across the world. 'Let me know when you arrive and how every-thing—'

But Maeve was already turning away to join the stream of travellers on the way to Customs. Only as the doors closed behind her did Corey wonder if she had done the right thing.

Lost in these thoughts, she didn't look where she was going and crashed into the tall man who had been standing behind her.

'I'm so sorry,' she said. 'I didn't see—' And she looked up to find herself staring into Mario's eyes, smiling down into her own as he caught her by the shoulders to steady her. Even though he was out and about at this early hour, he had taken the time to shave and she caught a whiff of his signature cologne. He was groomed to the point of elegance and wearing his trademark dark blue suit, making her feel scruffier than ever and at a complete disadvantage.

'What are you doing here?' they said in unison, making them both smile and get across what might otherwise have been an awkward moment.

'Seeing my parents off to Italy,' he said. 'They always visit the rellies at this time of year. And you?'

'Posting my sister to Paris,' she said, remembering too late that she wasn't supposed to be pleased to see him although her heart seemed to think otherwise, beating so strongly, she could feel it in her chest.

'I was so sorry to hear about your suspension,' he said. 'Tony said it was Smithson's fault.'

'The chief steward didn't think so,' she shrugged. 'I made a mistake and paid for it.'

'Six weeks is a bit tough.'

'I'll live,' she muttered, glancing at her watch and hitching her bag on her shoulder. 'Have to get going, Mario. No doubt I'll see you around.'

'Corey, don't rush off. Can't we talk for a moment?' He nodded towards the café not far away. 'Have coffee maybe?'

'Mario, what can we possibly have to say to each other? You've already made your feelings abundantly clear.'

'I made a mistake – it was wrong—'

'For us to spend the night together? Yes, it was. And I'll make sure it doesn't happen again.' So saying, she turned away, surprised to see the stricken look in his eyes. What could he possibly want with her?

'I was going to hire a limo to get back to town – can I offer you a lift somewhere?'

'No need.' She found herself able to speak only in short sentences. Just being close to Mario set her heart thumping so fiercely, she could hardly breathe. 'I have my car.'

'Then maybe you'll do me a huge favour and take *me* back to town? It can be the very devil, trying to get a limo or even a taxi at this hour.'

'Why not?' she shrugged, pretending indifference although her heart felt as if it were swooping up and down on a swing. Aware that he was watching her closely, she willed herself not to blush. 'But it won't be the luxury you're used to.'

'How do you know what I'm used to?'

'I can imagine.'

'All right, you're on. You can come and see my place right now. I'll make you breakfast.'

Corey said nothing, marching beside him to the car park. This really wasn't a good idea. Not having seen him for several weeks, she had almost succeeded in banishing him from her mind. Running into him unexpectedly had undone all that good work. She wanted him just as desperately, if not more than before. But if he thought of her as no more than a casual bedfellow to be taken up and dropped at will, he would soon find out otherwise.

She unlocked the doors and he got in – a large presence in her small car. Yet again she detected that wonderful lemony cologne, remembering that in the rush to get Maeve ready and out of the house, she had neglected to have a shower. She didn't expect him to remark on it.

'Girl sweat – salty and sweet.' He said, sniffing the air near her. 'With just the faintest smidgin of leather and horse. Very sexy. I like it.'

Not knowing what to make of him, she ignored the remark and concentrated on her driving instead, speeding up to join the stream of traffic on the freeway.

'You drive well,' he said after a while.

'How do you know? You've only been watching me for ten minutes.'

'You don't weave in and out of the traffic like some drivers – you don't change lanes unless you have a reason.'

'Must be my training as a rider – sometimes it's not all that different, you know.'

'And, unlike some girls, you know how to use the brake. You'd be amazed how many try to drive themselves out of trouble instead.'

'So I'll come to you, shall I? If I need a reference for a job as a driver?'

'Ouch!' He held up his hands in surrender. 'Didn't mean to sound patronizing.'

She smiled, pleased to have scored a hit.

She wasn't surprised when, after leaving the outskirts of the city, he directed her towards Toorak and through side streets so green and leafy, the trees almost met in the middle to make a solid canopy overhead. Just as she was thinking she'd never find her way out of this rat run, he told her to pull up outside a pair of imposing iron gates. Beyond was an impressive, double fronted house in red brick that must have been built around the turn of the previous century. Mario got out to open the gates and motioned for her to drive in.

'So this is your place?' she said, trying to sound as if she visited such mini palaces every day of her life.

'Some of the time,' he said. 'When I go overseas for more than six months, I rent it out.'

'Rent it out?' Momentarily, Corey was appalled. 'But you can't—'

'Not to people like Wendy.' He read her mind, laughing at her concern. 'But there are lots of visiting diplomats who like to borrow somebody's home for a short while rather than rent a hotel suite.'

'I didn't know,' she said in a small voice. So this was his home. Even Tony and Pat's renovated mansion paled in comparison. Wide steps led up to a double front door with two beautiful, stained glass panels on either side, depicting spiky Australian bottle brush and fairy wrens with their distinctive plumage in tones of navy and forget-me-not blue. He opened the door to reveal a narrow hallway furnished with genuine antiques – bronze tigers and horses in front of a huge ormolu mirror. Beyond this, a carpeted cedar staircase stretched away to the rooms above. The original early electrical light fittings had been restored and the house smelled of fresh furniture polish.

'Who looks after all this?' she whispered, half expecting a Victorian housekeeper to appear and order the stable girl round to the back door.

'You don't have to whisper. There's nobody here but us. I have a lady who comes in twice a week to keep it ship shape. Otherwise, I look after myself. Now for breakfast!' he said, ushering her into the kitchen – not an Edwardian kitchen of course, except for flagstones on the floor and the pine table with cottage chairs in the middle, but a modern renovation with solid wooden cupboards fitted around a gas stove, dishwasher and fridge.

'Sit down,' he said, taking off his coat and hanging it on the back of one of the chairs. 'I hope you like scrambled eggs, they're my specialty. Coffee?'

Suddenly, Corey felt less than happy. This was way too companionable and cosy. Although he was talking now as if they were friends and he really liked her, she would be just as quickly forgotten as soon as she left. It would be out of sight, out of mind once again and this time the hurt would be even greater. So she stood up again, deciding to leave.

'Mario, it's OK. You don't have to make breakfast for me. I really ought to get going. I told Tony I wouldn't be late and he'll be expecting me.'

'You're not driving all that way on an empty stomach.' He went on assembling his pots and lighting the stove. 'If you want to speed things up, you can make the toast.'

She did so, glad to be given something to do.

It was only when he set a plate of fluffy scrambled eggs in front of her,that she realized how hungry she was.

'Tuck in,' he said, scarcely able to wait for her, being ravenous himself.

'And you've done something else to them – something

delicious.' She chewed experimentally, trying to identify the taste.

'Scrambled eggs de-luxe with smoked salmon. I remembered how much you like fish.'

'Where did you learn to cook like this?'

'My uncle has a restaurant but he always says the simplest dishes are best. I make a good bruschetta with roasted capsicum, too.'

The coffee was delicious as well – hot and strong, just what she needed. But at last the meal was over and once more she stood up, murmuring that she should leave.

'But you've only seen the hall and the kitchen. I thought you wanted to see where I live?' And, ignoring other vague protests, he opened the back door to show her what was outside. 'There's a kitchen garden but I don't really have it maintained. A chap comes around once a month to cut the grass and deal with the weeds.'

'What a shame.' Corey looked out at the empty vegetable patch and neglected raspberry canes. 'There's nothing nicer than produce from your own garden.'

'Well, maybe if I had a – if I was here all the time,' he corrected quickly, and steered her along a corridor to see the rest of the downstairs rooms. She knew he had been going to say *if I had a wife* and she knew that he'd had one once but it hadn't worked out. A marriage arranged by their parents. Even at the time it had struck her as odd. Mario wasn't the type to submit to anyone arranging anything about his life. And, as for this house, it didn't seem like a home at all. Aside from the kitchen, it seemed more like a museum!

This impression was confirmed when he opened a door to show her a formal dining-room – a huge silver epergne in the middle of a massive dining table which had to be solid cedar, surrounded by twelve antique chairs – landscapes on the walls in ornate gold frames. It even smelled musty and put her in mind of a Victorian board room; she could just imagine a dozen grumpy old men sitting around it smoking cigars. Next door was a parlour that would have done justice to Jane Austen. There were antique Italian tapestries on the walls, a chaise longue and several other equally uncomfortable chairs with legs so thin they looked as if they might break if she sat on one.

'But you can't live in rooms like these,' Corey blurted without meaning to voice her thoughts so tactlessly. 'They look like something owned by the National Trust.'

'Thanks a lot,' he said, raising his eyebrows.

'Oh, I didn't mean that the house isn't lovely – it is. It just doesn't look as if somebody lives in it, that's all.'

'So Madame is determined to see the lion in his den? To do that, I'm afraid she must go upstairs.' He indicated the cedar staircase. *Stupid, Corey*, she thought, scolding herself. *You walked right into that one.*

Rescue came in the form of the hall clock striking eleven.

'Good heavens,' she carolled. 'Is that really the time? Mario, thank you so much for the breakfast but I really do have to—'

But he was already striding away up the stairs, expecting her to follow. Goodness only knew what would happen if she did. She was indeed about to enter the lion's den. He would show her his bedroom – his bed! *Don't even think about the bed!* She warned herself. He might be able to read your mind.

'Come on,' he grinned at her over his shoulder. 'I'm not going to eat you.' He *was* able to read her mind! 'If you want to see where I really do live – you have to come up here.'

Slowly, she walked up the stairs as he bounded ahead.

At the top of the stairs in one direction she saw a large bathroom, renovated in black marble. On the opposite side was a cosy sitting room with comfortable lounges positioned around a home theatre system. The walls were painted a neutral cream and the warmth in the room came from drapes and furnishings in soothing colours of dark red, russet and gold. Still the same antique theme but more liveable this time. A bookcase filled with books occupied the whole of one wall. She could see a small annexe beyond, containing his desk and computer.

The second room had to be his bedroom. And, much as she expected, it was clean and orderly as he was – no clothing strewn on chairs and the floor as in her room. She bit her lip remembering that he had spent the night in her own untidy abode.

A big handmade patchwork quilt lay across the largest bed she had ever seen. He must have to have linen specially made for it. On one side of the room was a mirrored built-in robe for his clothes and shoes. The room displayed only one picture, positioned on the opposite wall so that he could see it while lying in bed. Naked ladies of course with milk-white bodies and flowing seaweedy hair. Corey recognized the style of Klimt but it wasn't one of the more famous ones and she couldn't remember seeing it before. Not an original, surely?

'No, it isn't,' he said, once more reading her mind. 'Just a gallery print. But a good one from the Klimt Museum.'

'It's lovely,' she said, moving forward to examine it more closely. 'Klimt has always been a favourite of mine – his attention to detail and amazing use of colour.'

'So,' he said, placing his hands so gently on her shoulders, she scarcely registered that he had done so, although she was very aware of his tall presence behind her. 'A love of Klimt,' he said softly. 'Yet another thing that we have in common.'

Any moment now, she knew he was going to kiss her. But how was she to respond? Her sensible self told her to turn on her heel, go down that staircase and out of the house. But all her instincts were telling her otherwise; to leap into his arms, wrap her legs around his hips, bury her fingers in his hair and kiss him until they fell together on that wonderful bed. But, reminding herself what had happened the last time she had followed her natural instincts, she knew how unwise that would be.

'Please, Corey,' he whispered, sensing her tension. 'Don't shut me out. I don't want to lose you again.'

'You didn't have to lose me the first time,' she said more sharply than she intended. 'The choice was yours and you made it.'

'You don't understand—'

'No, Mario, listen. I can't do this. Because I made the mistake of sleeping with you before, you see no reason why it shouldn't happen again. But I can't – not now. It just doesn't feel right.'

'Corey—'

'No, let me finish. You're Italian and it's in your nature to be hot-blooded and want more than I am willing to—'

'Oh?' He moved into her space, crowding her. 'And you are so cool, so composed are you? My little Irish girl?'

As she slipped away under his arm to prevent him from seeing just how much he affected her, her attention was caught by a photograph of a girl in an ornate silver frame. It was standing next to a table lamp on the chest of drawers close to his bed.

'And who's that?' She turned to face him. 'Another girl-friend?'

His reaction was so swift and immediate, it startled her. He snatched up the photograph and shoved it face down into the top drawer of the chest. Having done so, he leaned back against it as if to prevent her from opening the drawer to look at it again, although he must know she wouldn't do any such thing. His mood had changed so quickly, she could only stare at him in amazement, at a loss for words.

Before either of them could speak, his mobile rang, breaking the tension between them.

'Yes?' he snapped, answering so fiercely that Corey was glad she wasn't the person at the other end of the line. 'Thank you, Serena,' he said crisply. 'I'll be there in ten.' He switched off, looking at and through Corey as if he didn't really see her at all, his mind running on something else.

'My father's P.A.' He said at last. 'Sorry to cut short your visit but I'm needed at the office,' he said. 'Lot to do with the old man away.'

'That's OK,' she said slowly. Was he schizophrenic or

what? Only a moment ago he had been making romantic overtures. Now it seemed that he couldn't wait to turn her out of his bedroom, out of his house. 'I should have been on my way half an hour ago.'

How had it happened? Once more the barriers were up, every word they uttered only adding to the distance between them. They were making all the right noises but saying nothing, like a pair of strangers being polite.

Reliving those last few moments, she was sure it wasn't the phone call from the office that unsettled him. It was the photograph he kept at his bedside; the photograph he must look at last thing at night and first thing in the morning.

The photograph he had hidden rather than let her see.

She wished she had looked at it more closely now. Was it his ex-wife or some other girl? Well, she certainly wasn't going to find out now.

Downstairs, he ushered her out of the front door and locked it behind them. While she got into the car and started it, he opened the gates to let her drive out, coming to the driver's side window to say good-bye. She wound it down to hear what he had to say.

'Corey, I . . .' he began, his extraordinary pale eyes troubled as they looked down into her own. Once again her heart gave its usual dance and she sensed he wanted to offer some sort of explanation for his behaviour.

'Yes?' she whispered, prompting him.

'Nothing,' he said at last, thinking better of it. 'Take care driving home. I'll be seeing you.'

She nodded, unable to speak for the rising lump in her throat. Somehow she managed to force a bright smile as she drove through the gates, sounding the horn as she increased speed, deliberately disturbing the peace of that quiet street. When she had travelled a few hundred yards, she stopped the car and rested her head on her hands at the top of the steering wheel. She had to because she couldn't see for the tears filling her eyes. *This is the last time* she told herself, after finding a tissue and blowing her nose, *the very last time I let that man into my life.*

After she'd gone, Mario walked slowly across the gravel towards his own car, housed in a carport at the side of the house. There *were* things to deal with at the office but there was nothing so urgent that it couldn't wait.

How had it happened? Yet again Corey had found her way into his life, amusing him, getting under his skin. And what would she think of him now? Inviting her for breakfast, insisting she stayed when she had told him more than once that she wanted to leave. He had been so close to putting things right between them. And then, just because she had dared to inquire about that photo of Rina, he had almost thrown her out of the house!

How could he explain that he was doing it for her own good? To save her from heartbreak? Once before he had tried to shut the door on his feelings for Rina. It hadn't worked. Perhaps because there had been no definite closure. His mother and father had told him she was dead and his rational self believed it. Unfortunately, because it had happened so suddenly and while he was away – he didn't even get home in time for the funeral – his subconscious couldn't let go.

In shock and not really caring what happened to him, he

111

had allowed himself to be married to Anna. At the time it seemed to be what everyone wanted and it didn't matter to him. In his heart of hearts he had known it was far too soon and would end in disaster. It did.

Although Anna found him presentable and wealthy enough to make a suitable husband, it wasn't long before she found out about his attachment to Rina.

'In love with your cousin,' she had sounded scornful as well as dismissive. 'That's disgusting.'

After that, she told him to his face that she didn't love him and never would and he discovered she was capable of loving only herself. She didn't even try to meet him half way. Born and raised in Rome, steeped in Italian fashion and culture, she never embraced the Australian lifestyle and disliked speaking English. And when she found him staring with tears in his eyes at that same photo of Rina – the one he had hidden from Corey – it was the last straw – she had the excuse she needed to leave.

And Corey – his heart still lifted at the thought of her – brave, funny and sexy as well – a natural, healthy girl who didn't have to look at herself every time she passed a mirror. That alone made her as different from Anna as it was possible for a woman to be. But that didn't mean things wouldn't turn out badly again. He was halfway in love with her – he knew that already – but was he prepared to put the past behind him and move on?

At the office Serena, his father's P.A. greeted him with a sheaf of printed emails and messages.

'Give me the most urgent,' he said. 'I'll deal with them first.' He turned away, heading for his office.

Serena watched him go, admiring his easy stride in that immaculate suit and let go a small sigh as she imagined what he would look like without it. But she knew better than to travel too far down that path. More than one girl in the office had broken her heart against the flint of his indifference. Mr Mario remained aloof, an intriguing enigma.

# CHAPTER SIX

COREY drove home in pensive mood. In hindsight, it was a good thing to have seen Mario in his own home, if only to confirm that there was no future for her with him. Compared to the loss of innocence and sense of betrayal she had felt after losing Jon, she had emerged from this latest encounter – too soon to call it a relationship – practically unscathed. She reminded herself yet again that she had a great opportunity at her feet – a career to think about. This wasn't the time to be diverted by a romance.

She made unusually good time getting home which made her realize with a pang of guilt that she must have been speeding. Maybe she did have more in common with Mario Antonello than she thought. And, as she was dressed in her riding clothes, ready for work, she drove straight round to the stables and parked her car alongside the others, including a big 4WD that wasn't familiar. Another new owner for Tony perhaps?

Inside, she wasn't best pleased to find that the visitor was Ray Mercer, the jockey whose place she had taken on Pirate.

Heads together and deep in conversation, he and Tony were discussing the horse as they watched him in his stall. Pirate, having finished his exercise for the day, was happily ignoring the men, devoting full attention to his feed.

As Ray saw Corey approaching, he concluded his conversation with Tony and clapped him on the shoulder, preparing to leave.

'We'll talk again old son,' he said. 'Jus' makin' the rounds to let everyone know I'm back in the saddle, lookin' for work.' He pressed a card into Tony's hand. 'Got a new agent, too. Good man. Call him if you can use me.'

'Thanks.' Tony accepted it. 'Never know. Got a lot going on.'

'Nice place you've got here. I'm impressed.' He gave Tony a conspiratorial wink before acknowledging Corey with more of a nod than a smile. 'Look forward to hearin' from ya, Tone.'

Corey folded her arms, watching him go, seeing that he still walked with a bit of a limp.

'What did he want?' she said.

'Oh, nothing. Just passing the time of day.'

'I suppose he wants *my* job?'

'Well, he can't have it, can he?' Tony said. 'He's too much of a prima donna, anyway – won't put himself out to do track work. But that's not to say I won't give him a ride now and then if it suits me.' He gave her a sideways glance, not quite sure how she'd take what he had to say. 'You know how I feel about you, Corey. You're good as a bloke, any day. But there are still some owners who'd rather see me put a man up.'

'The owner of Pirate King for one, I suppose?'

'Now then. You should know Mario by now.'

'I'm not sure I know him at all.'

'Well, he can't help his background, can he? It's ingrained – that old-fashioned protective instinct towards women. He still thinks Pirate's too dangerous for you—'

'And you're going to bow to his prejudice?'

'Only for now. My father used to say jockeys are rather like fruit – you have to take what's in season.'

'And being suspended, I'm out of season and Ray's in?'

'Lighten up. Only a few more weeks and you'll be back in the saddle.' Tony clapped his hands and rubbed them, his signal that the subject was closed. 'See Maeve on to the plane OK?'

'Yes. But now I'm wondering if we did the right thing.' Corey frowned, chewing her lip. 'I do hope Jon will be pleased to see her.'

'Why shouldn't he?' Being a straightforward man himself, Tony didn't look for complications in anyone else. 'He's her husband, isn't he?'

All the same, Corey continued to worry, especially when she didn't hear from her sister long after she should have touched down in Paris. She wished she had pressed Maeve for an address or even a telephone number instead of trusting her to make contact when she arrived. Now there was nothing to do but wait. The days of her suspension seemed longer than ever with this extra worry at the back of her mind.

So she threw herself into her work and, instead of leaving when the early morning exercising of the horses was done, she often stayed on to help out at the stables. One afternoon Tony caught her grooming Sequins.

'That's not your job, Corey. You've done enough for one day. Where's Terri?'

'It's all right, Tony, I offered to help. I like looking after Sequins.'

'That's not the point. Terri gets paid to groom horses and you don't. So where is she?'

'Outside, I think, taking a break. She won't have gone far.'

'Having a smoke, I suppose. She knows I hate anyone smoking near the stables – that's how accidents happen.'

He marched off and a few moments later Terri returned, looking mutinous and on the verge of tears. 'He says if I smoke around the horses again, he'll give me the sack. Did you *have* to tell him, Corey?'

'I didn't. He guessed.'

'Don't know why he makes such a big deal about it. Everyone used to smoke where I worked before.' She sighed, taking up a broom and raising a dust as she applied herself to sweeping the floor.

Banned from helping out in the stables, Corey spent most of her afternoons keeping fit by going for a gentle jog on the beach. In late autumn the heat had gone out of the sun and it was all but deserted, apart from one or two people with dogs and the occasional swimmer insane enough to brave the cold water.

Involved in the sense of well-being derived from her exercise, she didn't notice a tall figure striding towards her from the other end of the bay. Without his trademark business suit, she didn't recognize him at first, seeing only a man barefooted and wearing a polo shirt and pale jeans just like anyone else on the beach. Head down, lost in her own thoughts and the rhythm of running, she would have passed him without breaking her stride if he hadn't placed himself directly in her path and put out his hands to catch her. With a jolt of surprise that set her heart thudding, she realized it was Mario who held her.

For a moment, she was too breathless to speak. Why did he have to have this effect on her? Making her stomach feel as if it were full of butterflies, trying to escape. Why did he have to come to the beach at all, reminding her of the feelings she had for him; feelings that she had done her best to suppress?

'I think we'd better sit down,' he said, dropping full length on the sands and leaning back on his elbows. 'You must have done enough running for one day – you're red as a turkey.'

'Thanks,' she said, flopping down beside him 'You really know how to make a girl feel good about herself.'

He laughed, such a happy, infectious sound that she couldn't help but join in, watching his eyes crinkle as he smiled. What was she doing? She had promised herself that the next time she saw him, she'd keep a tight rein on her emotions and wouldn't fall for his particular brand of charm. In casual clothes, he looked younger, more carefree, the tight polo shirt defining his muscular chest and strong arms, reminding her all too vividly how they had felt holding and touching her as they made love. Thinking of *that* wasn't going to help her red face either.

'You're looking well,' he said. 'Very relaxed. Being suspended suits you.'

'If you must know, it doesn't suit me at all. I'm going stir crazy away from the track.' She gave him a sideways glance, unable to resist a small dig. 'Where have you been? We haven't seen you for weeks.'

'Blame my father. He's a very 'hands on' CEO. There's always a lot to take care of when he's away.'

'So what brings you here today?'

'Important business with Tony – firming up a deal on the two mares we're importing from Ireland. Our first breeding stock.'

'But this is a racing stables. Tony never said he was interested in breeding?'

'He isn't but I am. He has the contacts so he's guiding me through it, helping me to get started.'

Corey looked out over the water. 'I'd like to do that one day. I can't think of anything more satisfying than breeding a foal to grow up and win a Melbourne Cup.' She sighed. 'But I'll never have enough money.'

'Neither do I, at present – that's why we're starting small. Most of my money's tied up in the 'museum' as you call it. But it doesn't hurt to dream. Lots of good ideas come out of that.'

He stood up and sent a pebble skimming across the waves, watching it until it dropped. At the same time he was very aware that Corey was watching him closely. He had come to Mornington with the intention of telling her everything; his ill-fated love for Rina, his unfortunate marriage to Anna and to speak of a future which might include her. But now he was having second thoughts. Seeing her reminded him all too vividly of the scene in his bedroom – his fear that she would recognize in that picture of Rina, someone who looked too much like herself. Then it really would be over between them. Her temper was volatile – that was one of the facets of her nature that made her so interesting and exciting; placid women bored him. But it also meant she jumped to conclusions and might not give him time to explain. Would she stay still long enough for him to tell her that while her similarity to Rina had attracted him in the first place, he wanted her for herself?

And would she believe him when he said the past was behind him and he was ready to move on? Did he believe it himself? It had been ten years since he lost Rina and in Corey he had found her again. Or had he? After so many years, could he really remember exactly what Rina was like? The sound of her voice? Her laugh? Or had Corey somehow merged with the ghost and taken her place? A woman of flesh and blood he could hold in his arms instead of a shade from the past who haunted his dreams with a false reality, only to vanish in the morning leaving him bereft.

But would she believe he wasn't still trapped in the past? The evidence against him was all too damning; keeping that picture of Rina beside his bed. In the end he decided to leave well alone and keep his secrets to himself.

He sent several more pebbles skimming across the water but they didn't help him to think straight at all. She stood up and came to stand beside him, throwing a pebble of her own.

'How's your sister?' he asked, changing the subject. 'Enjoying her stay in Paris?'

'I have no idea,' she said, her expression clouding. 'I made her promise to call me when she arrived but I haven't heard a word.'

'She didn't leave an address?'

'No and, like a fool, I didn't ask for one.' She sighed. 'No news is good news, I suppose.'

'You don't sound very sure?' He sent another pebble skimming across the water, wondering whether to tell her what he knew about Jon or not. In the end he decided against it. He gave a shout and punched the air as the pebble sliced through at least six waves before it dropped. 'There! That was a good one. Did you see it?'

She ignored the question. 'Mario, you didn't come here just to throw pebbles or ask after my sister—'

'No, I didn't,' he said lightly. 'I came to see you.'

'Why? Because after the last time we met—'

He dropped the next pebble and surprised her by pulling her into his arms. 'Mm, you smell lovely.' He said, burying his face in her neck. 'Shampoo, horses and girl sweat.'

'Stop avoiding the question.' She tried to push him away, only to find herself drawn more closely into his embrace. The man was exasperating! A chameleon of so many moods. Not only was it impossible to predict them but he had an uncanny talent for catching her at her worst. This had to be her oldest tracksuit and she must look like a scarecrow without any make-up and hair on end.

His mouth descended towards her and she knew he was going to kiss her but although she wanted it more than

121

anything, perversely she wasn't about to surrender without a fight. With a quick wriggle that had served her well, rescuing her from more than one tight corner in the stables, she was out of his arms and running away up the beach. As she knew her territory better than he did, she meant to tease him by running away and hiding in the thick under-growth on the foreshore. She was fast but she hadn't counted on his longer stride and shrieked in mock fright when she heard him gaining on her.

Moments later, he caught her, ready to bring her down in what might have been a painful rugby tackle, except he twisted at the last minute and threw himself down in front of her, using himself as a pillow to break her fall.

Even so, Corey felt the breath knocked out of her body as she landed heavily on top of him. Moments later she was greeted by the unmistakeable response of his arousal and instinctively parted her legs to feel him against her more closely. Then the kissing started, greedy and breathless as if they couldn't get enough of each other, his stubble grazing her chin, raising her heart rate and turning her weak with desire. She buried her fingers in his thick hair to draw him still closer. The bush all around them was prickly and uncomfortable but she was scarcely aware of it. They could have been lying on a nest of scorpions and she wouldn't have cared.

He rolled over with her and pulled down the zip of her tracksuit top, giving a soft growl of pleasure as he saw exactly what he suspected, that she was wearing nothing at all underneath it. Still kissing her but more gently now, he started touching her breasts with his fingertips, circling her

122

nipples and pinching them until they were hard and erect. Lost to sensation, she moaned softly, feeling an answering stab of desire deep inside her, making her arch towards him. How could such a big man have such sensitive fingers? When her nipples were fully engorged, he took each into his mouth in turn, making her sigh with pleasure and adjust her position to fit herself around his swollen member although they were still fully clothed.

'Now,' she urged him, her voice husky with passion. 'Do it now, Mario. I can't wait any longer.'

But instead of plunging inside her to bring the release she craved, she heard him pause and swear softly, patting his pockets.

'What's wrong?' she whispered.

'I have no protection. They're still in the top pocket of my suit.'

'Not a boy scout, then?' she said ruefully, wondering how to live with this aching need that seemed so totally to possess her. She didn't have to wait long. He bent to kiss her throat and teased her breasts with his palms before sliding his hand under the waistband of her tracksuit to rest on her belly.

'Oh no,' she groaned. 'Mario, I can't stand it. Don't tease me any more.'

'Trust me, darling. I won't,' he whispered, and slid two fingers inside her as if he already knew how moist she would be, how aroused.

She stiffened at first, unwilling to give herself up to such selfish pleasure until he reassured her by kissing her deeply again and moving his fingers inside her to find the seat of her desire, seducing her into clenching herself around it to join his rhythm with a more urgent one of her own. At the same time, she was a little shocked that he should know so exactly how and where to touch her, to bring her to orgasm so readily. And what now? Would he despise her for being so needy, so lacking in control that she would let him satisfy her in that way? Her heart gave a lurch as she froze, waiting to see if he would turn away from her yet again.

'You are amazing,' he said at last, pushing the hair away from her face and kissing her more tenderly this time, looking into her eyes that were still languid with passion. 'A woman without inhibitions – perhaps because you are so in tune with horses and nature. I've never met anyone quite like you before.'

And even as he was saying it, he realized it was true, She was really nothing at all like Rina who had always blushed when he saw her naked and felt shame when she let him make love to her. They had both been so achingly *young*.

The sun was slipping away fast now and the afternoon getting cool. He pulled up the zip of her tracksuit and assisted her to her feet, brushing the sand from her clothes. 'This really has been a stolen afternoon. I have to get back to town.'

'You have to go now? Tonight?' She said, feeling her heart sink with disappointment as they started to walk back in the direction of the racing complex. 'I was hoping you'd stay.'

' 'Fraid not.'

He heard her shuddering sigh and stopped, turning her

to face him, seeing the quivering lips and the hot tears starting in her eyes.

'What's this?' he said, gently kissing her trembling lips, 'I didn't say I was going alone. I want you to come with me. I have to collect my messages and make a few phone calls. And after that, I'll take you to dinner. We need to talk.'

'What about?'

He gave her a lazy smile and traced a finger down her nose to rest on her lips. 'Everything.'

'And then?'

'We'll see what develops, shall we?'

Seeing the thinly veiled desire in his eyes, she felt an answering ache deep inside her all over again. But would she be able to do this? Could she really spend the night in his room with that photograph? The memory of it would plague her, even if it remained out of sight.

'I'll have to square it with Tony,' she said, before accepting his offer. 'I don't want to take too much time off. Ray Mercer's already hanging around and breathing down his neck.'

'Be sensible, Corey. We need him. A stable can't rely on only one jockey.'

'Especially if that jockey happens to be female.' She lifted her chin defiantly, sensing the way the conversation was leading.

'Calm down. I've asked Tony to engage someone else to ride Pirate, that's all. It takes nothing away from you.'

'Oh? I'd say it was just the thin end of the wedge.'

He made an impatient gesture. 'Corey, don't stress about it. After all, it's only a job – and a dangerous one at that.'

She sighed, raising her eyes heavenwards. 'Just as I was beginning to think you understood.'

'I do. I know very well how *you* feel but you refuse to see my point of view. If you could have seen yourself as I did today. Relaxed, free of tension and with a wonderful bloom about you – almost womanly.'

'Oh, no.' She ran her hands down her thighs. 'It doesn't show on the scales but d'you think I'm putting on weight?'

'Listen to yourself. You sound like Ally Smithson. As if nothing matters but riding and winning a race. Well, I have news. That's not living a full life, it's only a part of one. So what are you going to do? Keep on riding for years until you're dried up and wizened as Smithson?'

'I don't know.' She didn't want to answer these uncomfortable questions. 'I haven't thought that far ahead.'

'Well, think about it now, before it's too late.' His eyes were shooting sparks and she knew he was getting angry although she didn't really understand why.

'Mario, stop this. Don't pick a fight with me now: Not on such a beautiful day.'

'All right, I know. I'm a brute.' He let go a long breath, putting an arm round her shoulder and pulling her close. 'But I can't bear the thought of you putting yourself in danger – getting hurt.'

'But I love riding – it's what I was born to do. And I'm not going to get hurt.'

He kissed her then; a gently searching kiss not entirely devoid of passion. She knew he wasn't entirely happy but she didn't know what to do about it. Afterwards, she leaned against him, looking across the sea at the sun slowly descending on the horizon, painting the sky with flame that was a shimmering golden reflection in the water below. They watched it until the colour was gone and the sun had all but disappeared.

Back in her apartment, Corey rang through to Tony to ask if he needed her the following morning.

'Nope,' he said. 'You've worked damned hard these last few days and deserve a bit of time off. We've got prospective owners coming for Sunday lunch so we won't be doing too much on the track in the morning.'

Corey relayed this message to Mario and gave him a newspaper to read while she took a shower.

'It'll save time at the other end if I take one with you—' he said, looking disappointed when she shook her head. 'S'matter? Don't you trust me?'

'Absolutely,' she said cheerfully. 'I'm the one I don't trust – and I know you don't have any condoms.'

'Don't *you*?'

'What are you thinking?' She pursed her lips in a parody of Eliza Doolittle. 'I'm a good girl, I am.'

'Are you, indeed? Tell that to the man who was taking snaps of us in the bushes.'

'What?' She stared at him, feeling the colour drain from her face.

'Only joking.' He laughed and ducked as she threw a cushion at him on the way to the bathroom, taking with her the clothes she would wear that evening and also making certain she locked the door. She wasn't sure if she was disappointed or relieved when he made no attempt to intrude. When she emerged fifteen minutes later, fully dressed in jeans and a figure-hugging pink sweater, he was sitting exactly where she had left him, engrossed in the paper.

He looked up and smiled. 'You look great,' he said, making her flesh tingle as his gaze flickered over the plunging neckline. 'Good enough to eat. I don't think I've seen you in pink before.'

'I don't often wear it,' she said. It had been a present from Maeve and she had never felt confident enough to show off her figure in such a provocative garment. But it felt right for tonight, along with a pair of matching pink crystal ear rings that brought a sparkle to her eyes.

But thinking of Maeve revived all her recent anxieties. Her sister must have arrived in Paris more than a week ago. Why hadn't she heard from her? Hopefully, she was so happy with Jon that she had forgotten her promise to keep in touch. Somehow Corey had the feeling that this wasn't so.

In Mario's powerful car and using the motorway, they reached the outskirts of the city in no time at all and moments later were pulling up outside the 'museum.' While Corey sat in the kitchen, toying with a glass of iced water, he checked his messages and made a phone call to his favourite restaurant, spending several minutes being blatantly charming and pulling strings to get a good table. Then he ran upstairs to change. Ten minutes later he reappeared – shaved, showered and wearing his trademark dark blue suit. Corey also caught a whiff of that now familiar Tuscan cologne.

'What is that wonderful stuff?' she murmured. 'It does things to me.'

'It's supposed to,' he whispered, ushering her out of the front door. 'But we don't have time now. We have to be there in ten or we'll lose that table.'

'Are you sure this is good enough for a fancy place?' She bit her lip, glancing down at her casual clothes. Mistakenly, she had expected him to stay in his jeans.

'It's only a seafood bistro on the beach,' he said. 'Or it was before it became the darling of the 'in' crowd. Service is pretty relaxed and the food's good. That's all that matters.'

At the restaurant, Mario was greeted like an old friend by the host who remembered to ask after his parents by name. Corey received a polite smile and a raised eyebrow which Mario didn't see. Clearly, the man was used to seeing him with more glamorous girls.

One of the best tables had been saved for them and soon they were seated in comfortable basket chairs around a scrubbed pine table in front of the full length windows overlooking the beach. Palms waved in the evening breeze, a lighthouse flickered at one end of the bay while the lights of the city twinkled and lit up the sky with an orange glow at the other.

Water was brought to the table and home made bread and dips served by waiters wearing oversized aprons in the French bistro style. Mario ordered a bottle of Chandon and then they were left to study the menu.

'The barbecued prawns are good,' he advised, 'with special garlic chips. And their sweets are to die for – we have to leave room for those.'

'The prawns, yes. Not so sure about pudding.' Corey was looking at the menu rather than into his eyes as she spoke. 'I'll be back in the saddle, watching my weight again soon.'

Fortunately, at that moment, the champagne arrived before he could comment. Vintage Australian Chandon – sparkling bubbles of rose to match Corey's pink sweater.

'To be accurate, we must call this a sparkling wine, not champagne,' he said. 'But it's made by the same people and under the same conditions as in France.'

Corey smiled, about to take a sip from her glass.

'Wait a moment – we need to make a toast,' he said. 'To a better understanding between us.'

'To us,' Corey echoed, hoping he didn't expect all the compromise to be on her side.

Before they could finish their glasses of Chandon, the barbecued prawns arrived. Surprisingly huge, they had been cut in half, spiced and flattened for a quick turn on the barbecue before being served with roasted chunks of potato and whole cloves of garlic, a fresh green salad on the side.

Once again, Corey found she was starving and able to do justice to the delicious meal. Afterwards, she wouldn't let Mario order sweets although he insisted that they must have coffee accompanied by the restaurant's hand made chocolate truffles.

'So.' He sat back, after pouring her a second glass of delicious, sparkling wine, declining any more for himself because he was driving. 'What do you think has happened to your sister?'

Once more, Corey felt a jolt of unease at the mention of

Maeve. All the same she gave him a sketchy version of what had happened, neglecting to mention Jon's debts and the phone calls from his creditors clamouring to be satisfied.

'And you're worried about her?'

'Yes, I am. Because Jon is so – so—' she bit her lip, searching for a word that wouldn't be too damning.

'Unreliable?' he put in.

'Yes. So you do know something about him?'

' 'Fraid so. Everyone knows who's who in the fashion world and, for a little fish, Jon Manolito makes a lot of waves. Did your sister mention that he was trying to sell out to my father?'

'No. No, she didn't,' Corey said slowly, putting down her wine glass to stare at him. Suddenly, he had all her attention. Maeve, repeating Jon's version of events, had told her a very different tale. That Guido Antonello was a shark – a corporate raider – pursuing and threatening Jon for refusing to part with his exclusive and lucrative business. In the light of what she now knew, Mario's version seemed much more like the truth.

'My father looked at it, of course – he looks at everything – but the old man is shrewd and didn't come down in the last shower of rain. He smelled a rat but he gave it to the accountants anyway, to make sure. They told him the sums just didn't add up so he declined Jon's offer, without regret.'

'Jon wouldn't like that.'

'No, indeed. He was pretty insulting. Called my father a mafia boss, a crook who had wasted his time and promised to ruin our reputation in Melbourne. Of course, the only reputation he ruined was his own.'

'He owes money all over town,' Corey blurted at last and went on to describe that uncomfortable last evening with the telephone ringing all night.

'You should have left the answering machine to deal with it.'

'Maeve said it was broken and she couldn't afford to replace it. And we had to keep answering the phone in case it was information about her flight. She was absolutely stony when I last saw her and hadn't been eating properly since Jon left. He told her the show in Paris had been a success but she never saw any money from it. It's as if he'd totally forgotten he *had* a wife.'

Mario frowned. 'So he didn't know she was coming? He didn't expect her?'

Corey shook her head. 'She was so desperate to get over there, I paid for her plane ticket and lent her some money to go on with. Now I'm wondering if we did the right thing.'

'Well, it's either all right or all wrong.' Mario sat back to think, acknowledging the arrival of the coffee and truffles. 'I have family in Paris – my mother's younger sister, married to a doctor. When Maeve finally gets in touch, you can give her their address. I'll send them an e-mail so they'll be expecting her call. Then at least she'll have a bolt hole if she needs one.'

'Thank you. That would be a great relief.'

Having done their best to solve that problem, they gave their full attention to the truffles, Corey closing her eyes almost in ecstasy as the smooth, delicious chocolate melted in her mouth.

'You're easily pleased.' He gave her such a warm smile it made her heart seem to turn in her chest. 'I must remember that.'

'I don't have chocolate all that often. It's one of my weaknesses.'

'And the others?' he said, taking her hand and turning it over to kiss her palm, making her shiver.

'I think you've found them already,' she murmured, in a voice that wasn't quite steady.

# CHAPTER SEVEN

I T was only after they left the restaurant and went for a walk along the beach in the moonlight that Corey realized they had spent the whole evening talking of everything and everyone except themselves. Was that accidental or had Mario skirted the issues on purpose? She didn't know. But now wasn't the time to thrash out any serious differences; not with a bright, full, autumn moon overhead and the sea whispering softly in the distance. It was easier just to stroll with their arms around each other, toes scuffing the cool, shifting sands, their shoes dangling from the free hand.

When they came to the pier, they put on their shoes to walk out over the water, enjoying the sound of the sea sloshing around the barnacle-encrusted supports beneath. Always busy in daylight hours, tonight it was deserted apart from one or two dedicated fishermen, apparently content to catch nothing. The breeze freshened and the waves increased as they walked further out over the sea and Corey, chilled now, folded her arms across her chest in a vain attempt to keep warm. Immediately, Mario took off his jacket and draped it around her shoulders. Thanking him with a look, she almost purred like a cat as she hugged it around her, breathing in the warm masculine scent of him as well as the now familiar Tuscan cologne.

'But what will *you* do without it?' She smiled up at him. 'Shiver for your chivalry? Most boys my age wouldn't do this. They'd just tick me off for not bringing a coat.'

'Well, if you see the old dotard turning blue from hypothermia, you'd better give it back. But I have a better idea. Lets go home now.' He took her hand and they ran all the way back to the car, arriving breathless and laughing.

At this time of night, with the theatres and restaurants turning out, the roads were busy, making the journey slow. Mario put on his favourite – La Boheme – on the stereo and Corey lay back, closing her eyes, once more allowing herself to be transported to another world by the music.

Back at the 'museum,' she offered to make some coffee while Mario went to take off his suit. But, instead of returning in a tracksuit, as she expected, he arrived in a black Chinese silk robe, wearing very little underneath it. While they were both aware they had come here expressly to make love, this rather blatant assumption touched a nerve and Mario sensed it.

'A drop of whisky to go with the coffee?' He picked up the bottle, offering it.

'No thanks,' she murmured. 'It would be a waste. I don't really like it.'

'You'll like this one. It isn't that rough stuff Tony keeps at the stables.'

'I'll have you know that's best Kentucky bourbon. Pat told me so.'

'That's as may be. But this is the real thing; vintage Dalwhinney, so smooth that, once you've tasted it, you'll never want anything else.'

'Just half a measure then. I don't want to waste it.'

'You won't.'

The whisky was just as smooth as he promised, aromatic on the tongue and making her think of remote Scottish lochs and rolling highlands covered in gorse and heather. And when he kissed her, his mouth tasted so pleasantly of the expensive liquor, she began to relax.

Lifting her into his arms and continuing to kiss her, he carried her slowly up the stairs and pushed open the bedroom door with his foot. But as soon as she found herself on the threshold of that room again, she tensed in his arms.

'All right. What is it? What's wrong now?' he said, setting her down on the floor, instead of joyfully tossing her on to the bed as he'd planned.

'The photograph?' she said through a sudden tightness in the throat. She had forgotten it entirely until he brought her into this room when all her initial hurt and curiosity came flooding back.

'What photograph? As you can see – there isn't one.'

'Not now. But there was when I came here before. A photograph of a girl. It was standing right there by your bed in a silver frame. And she must be someone important for you to keep it close to your pillow like that.'

'Well, it's not there now, is it?' He ground out the words. 'And even if it were, it has nothing to do with us. You don't need to know anything about her.'

'I'm sorry but I think I do. All right – I admit there's a certain – chemistry – between us and for some reason best known to yourself, you find me – desirable. But so far I've seen no evidence of real love. You told me your marriage to Anna was one of convenience and yet you keep her photograph right next to your bed.'

'That wasn't my ex-wife.' His eyes flashed dangerous sparks of steel.

'Oh? You have a mistress, then?'

'Corey, let it be. This won't do either of us any good. We came up here to make love—'

'You don't have to remind me. And I wanted it just as much as you – or I thought I did. But I can't push these doubts to the back of my mind, pretending they don't exist. There are too many secrets lying between us.'

'All right, then. What about *your* past? You must have one. You weren't a virgin when we made love the first time – and that's OK.' He spoke quickly to silence any protest. 'I wouldn't expect it. But I haven't demanded to know about your previous lovers, have I?'

'There was only one,' she said in a small voice. 'And you had only to ask.'

'I didn't want to – didn't need to. What happened before we met is just water under the bridge. We should let it lie. Corey, it's been a wonderful evening – don't ruin it, please.'

He took a step towards her as if he would smother her doubts with kisses. Instinctively, she took a step back away from him.

'Better to ruin one evening than the rest of my life. Because

137

the past isn't dead for you, Mario, is it? Not while that photo-graph means so much that you don't even want me to see it.'

He stared at her as if he couldn't believe what she had just said. Gradually, he mastered his temper, his mouth setting in a grim line, making him look older than his thirty-five years.

'You're right,' he said at last. 'It's hopeless, isn't it? Doomed from the start. I should have known. Just go now, Corey – go downstairs and wait for me. I'll get dressed and then I'll drive you home.'

'No need.' She could hardly speak through the gathering tightness in her throat. 'I can hail a cab in Toorak Road.'

'I said I'll drive you.' He was polite but remote, still hold-ing his temper in check. 'Can't have you wandering the streets at this time of night.'

She realized her legs were starting to tremble and she stiffened them, pressing her knees back so that he wouldn't see how upset she was. She couldn't afford to break down in front of him, not now. And worse, she knew she had no one to blame but herself. Nothing was ever perfect and she'd been a fool to expect it. He was older than she was and of course there were and might still be other women in his life. Why couldn't she just accept what he offered and try not to question it? Why did she have to spoil it by want-ing to know too much?

But there was still a small voice inside her head saying that if he were serious, he would want her to know all about him, leaving no doors closed. No relationship could thrive unless it was founded on trust.

He came down wearing a black sweatshirt over his jeans,

scarcely casting a glance at her as he ushered her into the car. With his face set in that implacable mask, she had no idea what he was thinking and didn't dare ask. Nor did she have the courage to warn him not to drive fast.

The Ferrari started with an obedient growl and Mario revved the engine, deliberately disturbing the peace of the neighbourhood, causing one or two dogs to bark and lights to appear in upper windows. When he paused for a second or two, letting it die down, she tried to reach him once more.

'Mario, I know you're angry with me but—'

'No Corey, I'm not angry with you.' He spoke softly and patiently – too patiently. 'I blame myself entirely. This isn't your fault – it's mine.'

So far as she was concerned, he was still speaking in riddles and would have said so but he cut off any further attempt at conversation by putting a CD in the stereo and turning it up full blast. No romantic opera this time but Mozart's Requiem – something dark and entirely suited to his mood.

Much as Corey expected, as soon as he picked up the motorway, he took the car into the fast lane, impatiently tail-gating and hunting up any driver who didn't change lanes to move out of his way. And, even over the deafening music, it wasn't long before she heard a siren blaring behind them and they were joined by an unmarked police car, the driver signalling to Mario that he wanted him to pull over on to the hard shoulder.

The plain clothes policeman climbed out of the car and came over, waving his badge. Mario snapped off the stereo to hear what he had to say.

'Licence and registration, please sir.'

With icy politeness, Mario produced them, while Corey stared out of the window, looking at nothing, hoping Mario would hold his temper long enough to avoid being arrested.

'You seem to be in something of a hurry, sir? Or do we think we're Michael Schumacher? He drives a Ferrari, doesn't he?' The young policeman almost rocked on his heels, enjoying his own laboured sense of humour.

'If you're going to give me a ticket, get on with it,' Mario snapped. 'I haven't got all night.'

'Have you been drinking, sir?' The next question came automatically. A breathalizer was produced and Mario asked to blow into it.

Corey tried to remember what he'd had. Only one glass of wine at the restaurant but he had taken a substantial shot of whisky back at the house as he wasn't expecting to drive again that night.

'Just under the limit, sir.' The policeman sounded almost disappointed. 'You're lucky. One more standard drink and you would have been over—'

'But I wasn't, was I?' Mario snapped back again. 'Perhaps, Officer, you'd tell me which particular law I've broken, do whatever you need to do about it and let us get on our way. I wasn't speeding, was I?'

'No, sir.' Once again the young policeman seemed disappointed. 'But you were leaving insufficient room between your car and the vehicle in front of you. Dangerous driving that could cause an accident or force the driver in front to exceed the speed limit.'

'I'm a good driver. I know what I'm doing.'

'If you'd seen as many accidents as I have, sir, you would know those are famous last words. I'm letting you go with a caution tonight, but—'

'Then you've delayed me for nothing, haven't you? Wasting my time and yours—'

'There's no need to take that attitude, sir. I can always find an excuse to arrest you. You'll spend the night in the cells – even if we do have to let you go in the morning.' He glanced across at Corey's pink sweater with its plunging neckline, his gaze never reaching her face. 'And I'm sure you have very different plans for tonight.'

Corey forced herself to smile at him. 'I'm sorry, Officer, this is all my fault, I—'

'No Corey, it isn't – it's mine.' Gently, Mario interrupted her. 'I put you at risk.'

'Lovers' quarrel, eh?' The young policeman took a step backward. He had no real reason to detain them and was starting to withdraw. He and his partner had seen the Ferrari up ahead and, to relieve the boredom of a quiet night, had taken a punt that the driver might be breaking some law. 'Drive carefully, eh.' He patted the roof of the vehicle, making Mario wince. 'Nice car.'

Mario pulled out into the traffic and moved into the middle lane, travelling at a sedate speed this time..

'Go on then, say I told you so,' he said. 'You know you want to.'

'Not at all,' she said lightly. 'It's just one of the drawbacks of having a smart car. I suppose that sort of thing happens all the time.'

'On average, once a month. Change the CD would you,

if you can reach it. I think we've both had enough of the darker side of Mozart for one night.'

Corey didn't answer. If this was the nearest thing to an apology she was to get for his schizophrenic behaviour, it wasn't enough. All the same, she found a Rachmaninov piano concerto, something harmless, once used as background music for an old movie. Satisfied with her choice, he hummed along with it and they travelled more companionably than when they started out. In spite of another evening of see-sawing emotions, Corey found the music relaxing enough to nod off, only waking fully when the Ferrari pulled up in the gravel outside the gatehouse.

He switched off the engine and turned to speak to her but she held up her hand to stop him before he could say anything.

'Mario, I said I can't do this and I meant it. I can't be in a relationship when I don't know where I am—'

'But—'

'No, let me finish. You blow hot and then cold and I just don't know how to handle it. You interfere in my working life – as I knew you would—'

'Interfere?' Already tense, he fired up immediately. 'How do I interfere? Just because I want a man to ride Pirate?'

'And that's only the tip of the iceberg. Admit it. You don't want me to race at all. You'd rather see me broken down to the status of stable girl.'

He stared at her and his temper left him. He had never thought of her situation from that angle before. 'I never wanted you humbled, Corey. I just wanted you safe.'

'My safety is *my* concern. You're smothering me with

yours. And, aside from all that, you're so secretive. There are issues you don't want to talk about. To do with your past.'

'Corey don't talk about them because – I can't—'

'All right – I respect it if that's how it is.' She sighed. Suddenly, she felt incredibly tired. 'But it also means you're not ready to let it all go and move on. I feel as if I'm watching a man with one leg in the boat and the other on shore. If you don't make a choice, and quickly, you'll fall in the water and drown.'

'You don't paint a flattering picture of me.'

'I don't mean to. So – what I'm trying to say – and not doing it very well – is that I think we should call it quits. We can't see each other any more.'

'Of course you'll see me. I shall be working with Tony.'

'All right then, as colleagues. But not as lovers. Perhaps not even as friends.'

'You can't mean that, Corey. Not after all we've—'

'Been to each other? That isn't a great deal, is it? A dinner date, a breakfast and a one night stand.'

'Don't cheapen it. It meant more than that and you know it. Much more.'

'Then let's leave it in the realm of 'if only,' shall we? It will be far less painful for both of us.' She turned away from him. Having said what she needed to say, she felt exhausted and ready to leave. He put an arm across to stop her from opening the door.

'Corey, please. Don't leave it like this.'

Gently, she removed his arm and opened the door to get out. 'G'night, Mario,' she said with a rueful smile. 'Have a nice life.'

She pulled her key out of her handbag as she hurried up to the door, not daring to look back in case he followed. Quickly, she let herself in and leaned back against it, closing her eyes against incipient tears but still convinced she had done the right thing. When she opened them, the first thing she saw was a flashing red light on the answering machine by the phone.

Mario didn't leave immediately. He couldn't. He stayed where he was, momentarily stunned by Corey's rejection, not only of himself but all that he stood for. Although, on reflection, it was no more than he deserved. And worse, he knew where he'd got the script – from his father. Guido Antonello was a kindly despot who loved his family and wanted only the best for them. Unfortunately, he thought he *knew* what was best for them, too. He could be domineering and selfish, as well as old-fashioned and Mario had inherited a full measure of all these traits. No wonder an independent spirit like Corey wanted no more of him.

He glanced at the flat where the lights were still on and wondered if it was worth making one last attempt to put things right. Humble pie wasn't a dish he was used to eating and it was probably far too late even for that. Slowly he turned the key in the ignition and the Ferrari sprang into life although, out of consideration for the horses and sleeping horsemen who must be awake in just a few hours, he let it idle quietly. He was just about to put it in gear and leave when the front door opened and Corey came flying down the steps towards him, calling desperately for him to wait.

So miracles did happen, after all. He pressed a button to

open the window and talk to her.

'Mario, thank God you're still here. I've just found a message from Maeve – I called her back.'

'Is she all right?'

'No. She isn't all right, at all. I'm sorry to ask you when you must want to get home but can you—?'

He was out of the car immediately, following her into the house. Inside, he looked around the room.

'Do you have brandy or something? You look as if you need it.'

'No, I never keep anything in the house. I don't drink when I'm riding.'

'Tea, then. You sit down while I make it.' *Damn* he thought. *There you go giving orders again.* Luckily, this time Corey didn't seem to mind.

He switched on the electric jug in the kitchen, found teabags and quickly brewed two mugs of hot, sweet, tea.

'There's milk in the fridge if you want it,' she called from where she was sitting. 'I like mine black.'

'Me, too,' he called back, stirring in a generous amount of sugar. Then he carried them in and sat down beside her. 'Tell me what's happened.'

'Maeve is in Paris. She said it took a long time to find Jon – he wasn't at the address he gave her. He's living with some Scandinavian and her three children – has a funny name – Astrid, that's it. Maeve said she didn't know if any of the children were his.'

'Nasty situation.' Mario winced. 'Don't suppose the girl-friend was too pleased when your sister showed up.'

'No. Maeve said it was weird, a bit creepy – Astrid didn't

seem to mind at all, even asked her to stay and make up a
– a—' Corey clicked her fingers, searching for the word.

'*Ménage à trois?*'

'That's the one. It sounds better in French. Maeve said
"no" right away but she did accept the spare room. Says she
had to – didn't have enough money to pay for hotels long
term.' Corey paused, shaking her head. 'I wanted to give
her more money but she wouldn't take it.'

'Never mind that now. Tell me what happened.'

'She knows she should come home but she's scared in
case she's hounded for Jon's debts.'

'Can't get blood out of a stone. If she has no money and
he won't give her any – end of story.' Mario shrugged.
'They'll have to write it all off.'

'Then she found out why they really wanted her to stay.
Jon wanted to cash in her plane ticket and grab the money.
She said if she wasn't going to use it, then the money
belonged to *me*. There was a huge row when Jon snatched the
ticket from her handbag and threw her out of the house.
Luckily, she had the sense to put her traveller's cheques in her
shoe or he'd have taken those as well, leaving her destitute.'

'A charmer, isn't he? So where is she now?'

'At a cheap *pension* near the airport. She gave me the telephone number and now she's waiting for me to tell her
what to do.'

'Right.' Mario was suddenly all business. 'Do you mind
if I use your phone to call my aunt in Paris? If I explain the
situation, I'm sure Isabella will help.'

'Feel free. I'd be so grateful.'

He took over the phone and Corey heard him speak

rapidly in both French and Italian, smiling and giving the thumbs up to Corey.

'Fixed,' he said. 'My aunt's husband, Dominic, is just finishing surgery and then they'll go to the hotel and fetch her. Dom has an idea how to get her plane ticket back, as well.'

'If Jon hasn't already cashed it,' said Corey gloomily.

'That might not be so easy as he thinks. If the ticket is made out in her name – she'll have to cancel it.'

'I'll ring Maeve now and tell her not to panic – that Dominic and Isabella will be there for her.'

'Glad to be of service.' He stood up, preparing to leave. 'Let me know how it all goes.'

'Wait. I'm sure she'll want to thank you in person.'

'She can write me a note,' he said tersely. 'I have to go. It's late.'

'No.' Corey felt a flash of irritation. 'You'll do as I say for once. Sit down until I've spoken to my sister and let her thank you properly.'

He shrugged and sat down again as Corey dialled the number of the French *pension* and asked for Maeve who answered so quickly, she must have been waiting by the phone. Obviously, there were tears at the other end as Corey explained that rescue would be at hand in just over an hour. Then she handed the phone to Mario.

'Hi,' he said. 'You'll like Isabella. To me she's always been the next best thing to my mother – they're sisters, you see, and very much alike.'

'I'm not at all like Corey,' Maeve sniffed, still tearful and sorry for herself. 'She's not nearly as stupid as I am. I don't know how to thank you, Mr Antonello.'

147

'Mario, please.'

'Mario, then. I don't know what I'd have done without you.'

'My pleasure,' he said, raising his eyebrows to see if Corey wanted to speak to her sister again. She shook her head. 'Hold tight. They'll be with you very soon.'

While he was speaking to her sister, Corey started wondering how to get him to stay. At the time she left the Ferrari, she had meant every word she said but she knew now it was too late. Her emotions were too deeply involved to just walk away. Her heart had decided, whether she liked it or not, to overrule her head. He carried a lot of baggage from the past, she knew that already. With Mario, it might not always be easy – she could suffer some hurt. But at least she would know she was alive. Without him, the rest of her life stretched in front of her, empty as a desert.

Was it such a bad thing that he was a confident, domi-nant male? Hadn't she turned to him in this time of trouble, rather than Tony or Pat? And although she had rejected him just a short while ago, meaning to cut him out of her life forever, he had responded immediately to her cry for help. He could just as easily have turned his back on her and driven away. She wouldn't have blamed him.

But once more he was on his feet and heading for the door.

'You're not going now, are you?' she said in a small voice, coming close to him.

'What reason to stay?' he said softly, lifting her chin with one finger so he could look into her eyes. 'You've had what you need from me, Corey. Your sister is safe. And you've

148

made it crystal clear that you want nothing more.'

'How do you know what I need? What I want,' she murmured. 'Must you always make things so difficult for me?'

'Why should I make them easy?' he whispered, catching her mood and bringing his lips closer to her own.

'Just kiss me. I don't want to think of the past or the future. Only tonight.'

He took her face in his hands and kissed her with infinite tenderness.

'Don't be gentle,' she urged, pushing her hands up under his sweatshirt to feel the taut muscles of his chest. 'I'm not made of porcelain – I won't break.'

He needed no second invitation, throwing off his own sweatshirt and then removing her provocative pink sweater and the lacy bra underneath. 'You don't need to wear these things,' he murmured. 'You're quite beautiful without.'

'I'm not Lady Godiva – I can't ride around naked.'

'Ssh,' he said. 'This isn't the time for jokes.'

He kicked off his shoes and carried her into the bedroom, ignoring the untidy, unmade bed and the clothes scattered on the floor.

Corey went to turn off the bedside light but he stopped her. 'I want to see you,' he said, his eyes growing dark with passion. 'To remember tonight as the real beginning of everything for us.'

She lay back, revelling in the delicious sensation of his lips travelling from her wrist to her throat and then to her breasts, already peaking in anticipation. When he paused for breath, she pulled his head close again and made him kiss

149

her again until she saw his eyes growing dark with passion.

The range of emotions they had been through that evening had brought them both to a peak of sexual awareness. He lay on his back and lifted her on top of him to enter her quickly, closing his hands on her breasts until she flung her head back in ecstasy, supporting herself with her hands on his shoulders. As they moved in unison, he kept watching her with eyes sleepy with desire, waiting for her release; he was a generous lover and wanted to match it with his own. When it came at last, she gasped and shuddered to her climax with a low moan and collapsed against him, feeling as if she had travelled to the stars, to the very brink of heaven yet again.

In the course of the night, they awoke and made love again, taking it slowly and sensuously this time, almost ritualistic in their control. Corey hadn't realized how much she knew how to give a man pleasure until she saw the look of surprise and joy in his eyes as she caressed him intimately, teasing him with her lips, her hands. *Now I know why it's called 'making love'* she said to herself *because I do love him now, I really do, although we've never made any real promises or vows.*

It was only later, when she went to the bathroom, that she remembered that they had allowed themselves to be carried away and forgotten all thought of protection.

Sunday was the first day they had entirely to themselves. After a lazy morning, spent taking breakfast back into bed, feeding each other toast with black cherry jam and then making love on the crumbs, they had nothing to do.

Just as they were finishing a makeshift lunch of salad and scraps from the fridge, Pat telephoned, asking them to come over for coffee and meet the new clients, two brothers in business together, who were thinking of transferring their horses to Tony's stables.

Leaving Tony, Mario and the two men to talk over coffee, Pat drew Corey aside, murmuring something about wanting her to see some new curtains. Corey was puzzled. As a rule, Pat never asked her opinion about such things. But upstairs in Pat's bedroom, she recognized them as being the same flowered chintz she had seen before.

'But these aren't new curtains—' she began, turning to Pat in surprise.

'I know. That was just an excuse to get you alone for a moment.' Pat closed the door firmly behind them. 'Corey, what are you up to? You told me it was all over between you and Mario? Yet, here you are—'

'I know that's what I *said* but he doesn't seem to take 'no' for an answer.'

'Perhaps you need to say it more forcefully.'

'And perhaps I don't want to.' Corey bit out the words. Really she wanted to say it was none of Pat's business but instead she stared out of the window, avoiding the older woman's penetrating gaze.

'I just don't want to see you hurt again, that's all. I know you're of age and think you're old enough to look after yourself but it was Molly's last wish that I should take care of you.'

'Now Pat, please don't go there – don't bring my mother into this.'

151

Pat knew that Corey's feelings were always fragile when anyone talked about her mother but this time she didn't back down. 'And if she were alive today I know she'd be warning you not to make yourself so – so available to this man.'

Corey turned to look at her then. 'You don't like him, then?'

'Whether I like him or not has nothing to do with it. And, just for the record, I do. He has always been very straight in his dealings with Tony and me.'

'Well, then—' All Corey wanted was to put an end to this uncomfortable conversation but Pat wasn't ready to let her go.

'Darling, you've led a very sheltered existence. Apart from the short time when you were in town with Wendy, your life has been spent around horses and horsemen. Mario comes from a world of fast cars, high fashion and beautiful women. A world that couldn't be more different from our own.'

Corey folded her arms. 'So what are you saying? I'm not good enough for him?'

'Oh no, Corey, not at all.' Impulsively, Pat hugged her. 'You're a wonderful girl, more than good enough for any man. Tony and I are so proud of all your achievements. But what I'm trying to say – and not doing very well – is that Mario might not see this affair in quite the same light as you.'

'I don't understand.'

'Oh, dear.' Pat bit her lips. 'I've never been clever with words.'

'Please, Pat. Just tell me what's worrying you.'

'All right, I'll do my best.' Pat took a deep breath. 'Marriages that last are not always built on – on passion.

152

The best ones are usually made between people from simi-
lar backgrounds – I once heard someone describe it as
living on the same moral grid. Although Tony comes from
a horse racing family and mine owned a general store, we
are both country bred and our values and outlook on life
are the same.'

'OK. But what does this have to do with Mario and me?'

'He's very taken with you, dear. Anyone can see that. But
if you make yourself too – *available*' – once more Pat took
refuge in that word. 'I'm afraid he'll see you as just a play-
thing, a mistress rather than a potential wife.'

Corey was stunned, feeling the colour drain from her
face. *Was that what Mario thought of her?* Swept away by the
intensity of his feelings which she thought to be genuine, it
hadn't occurred to her that he might see her as 'easy.' That
she might be no more to him than a novelty, a diversion; his
pursuit of her no more than a means of slaking his lust. Her
heart plummeted as she remembered that photograph he
kept by his bed and still refused to discuss. Whoever she
was, that must be the woman he truly loved.

'Corey, darling, you've gone so pale. Are you all right?'
Pat reached out towards her again but Corey flinched,
unwilling to be touched.

'I'm fine,' she murmured automatically and forced a
bright smile. 'Thanks for the pep talk – I probably needed
it. You've given me plenty to think about.'

Downstairs, the new clients were already at the front
door. Having finished their business with Tony and Mario,
they were waiting to say their farewells to Pat.

When they had left, Mario held up a set of keys and

jingled them, smiling at Corey. So far he hadn't noticed her bleak expression. 'Tony's offered us the boat for the afternoon. Fancy a spin?'

'Go on, Corey, you love being out on the water.' Tony backed him up. 'Be winter soon – we shan't have too many more afternoons like this.'

'Oh, Tony, I don't know—' she started to refuse, suddenly weary of everything and needing some time to herself.

'You look as if you could do with a spot of sea air. Put the roses back in your cheeks.'

Feeling as she did, she knew it would take a lot more than sea air to do that. But she gave in with good grace, knowing it would cause even more drama and speculation if she were to refuse.

'There are rods on board and some bait in the freezer,' Tony went on. 'You might even catch us a fish. You'll find windcheaters in one of the lockers in case it gets cold later on.' He seemed quite happy to think of them as a couple. Only Pat watched them with troubled eyes, not quite ready to give her blessing.

Although the sun was still shining brightly, it was cool out on the water and they were grateful for Tony's rather musty, fishy-smelling windcheaters. Mario found the rods and baited one up for Corey as well as himself and, in competitive spirit, they started to fish.

Corey was first to catch a small snapper – so undersized it had to be thrown back.

Just as she did so, Mario let out a gleeful yell. 'Look at that,' he said, indicating a handsome King George whiting, wriggling and flashing silver in the sunlight as he brought it aboard. It was large enough to make a good supper so they kept it and Corey then caught two more for Tony and Pat.

Having caught enough fish to provide a satisfying meal for everyone, they pulled off the smelly windcheaters and retreated to the cabin where there were rugs to keep warm. She wrapped one tightly around her and sat up on the bunk, hugging her knees.

'What's wrong?' Mario came and crouched in front of her, looking up into her eyes. 'You're very quiet. Apart from those few moments when we caught the fish, you've hardly said two words to me all afternoon.'

'It's nothing.' She shook her head and looked down at her hands, unable to confide in him. 'Nothing at all.'

'Don't give me that. Has Pat been playing the mother hen? All the bounce had gone out of you when you came down from her room. What did she say to get you so upset?' He captured her cold little hands and enveloped them in his warm ones. 'Corey, tell me.'

'I don't want to.' She tried to withdraw her hands but he wouldn't let go. 'It's embarrassing.'

'How can anything be embarrassing between us, sweetheart? We've seen every inch of each other's bodies.'

'Exactly. That's just it.' She felt a blush spreading up from her neck to suffuse her cheeks. 'Pat says I've been making myself too "available"—'

To her surprise, he gave a delighted laugh. 'Isn't she wonderful? Still living in the nineteenth century. So what are you supposed to do now? Suppress all the natural urges and wear a corset that fastens like a fortress to keep a man at bay?'

155

'Something like that,' Corey wasn't yet smiling. 'She says you live in a world of fast cars and beautiful women—'

'Yeah, I know,' Mario broke in. 'And goes on to say I won't respect you if I have too much of my wicked way? I've heard those songs before. My aunt and mother sing them to all the girls in our family. It's just a ploy old women use to keep daughters nice.'

At last Corey managed a tiny smile.

'I'll tell you something about beautiful women – and I should know, I've lived among models and divas all of my life. Some of them aren't all that beautiful, either – they just photograph well. Really, they're a bit like rare and exotic tropical flowers. They look good, smell wonderful and promise rare and exotic sex. But more often than not, they're a disappointment – so much in love with themselves, they have nothing left to give anyone else. On the other hand, you—'

'Are not in the least bit beautiful.'

'Did I say that? No.' He frowned at the interruption. 'You're always putting words into my mouth. If you must know, I find you the most intuitive, naturally sexy, most satisfying lover I've ever had.'

'Thank you, Mario, that's very nice to know. But you still haven't said one word about love.'

'Must I put it in words? Don't you already know?'

'I'd still like to hear it from you.'

'All right, then. Close your eyes.' He waited until she had done so and then he kissed each of her eyelids in turn. 'I love you, Corey O'Brien. More than that – I adore you – I really do.'

Won over at last, she withdrew her hands from his and clasped them about his neck to give him a long kiss to which he responded in full measure, exploring her mouth with his tongue, unfastening her shirt to tease her breasts again with those sensitive fingers, circling her nipples with his thumbs until they reacted, blossoming once more into hardened peaks.

Although there was only a single bunk in the cabin and the space confined, out here on the water they could make love without inhibition, knowing no one would hear. Afterwards, Corey felt weak with lassitude, her sensitized flesh burning as if she were running a temperature, her curls plastered to her head, wet with her own perspiration. The cabin was hot as if it were a sauna, the windows fogged and running with condensation.

Mario propped himself against the cushions as Corey lay back naked in his arms, looking down at her slender, lily white legs stretched out against the long brown length of his own.

'You look like a mermaid,' he whispered, his breath warm in her ear. His hands closed on her breasts again, making her shiver. She had been so long at this peak of sexual tension that he had only to touch her to make her whole body come alive. She turned and offered her lips for his kiss which was both tender and leisurely, without urgency this time.

After a while, he looked at his watch and sighed. 'We should go in. There are no lights on the boat and it will be dark soon. Besides, I'll have to get back to town. Monday tomorrow.' He reached for his clothes and tossed over her own.

'Don't remind me,' she murmured as she pulled them on quickly. 'I'll be up at dawn to put your horse through his paces.'

She felt him withdraw a little, tensing at these words.

'You're not still riding Pirate?'

'At track work – of course. That's my job.'

'But I told Tony specifically—' He paused and looked away, biting his lip, realizing he'd said too much.

'That the horse was too dangerous, too strong for me – I know.'

'Corey, listen to me.' He pulled her round to face him so that he could look into her eyes. 'I didn't realize the sheer size and strength of a thoroughbred till I owned one and stood close beside him. And Pirate is entire – a stallion, a potential killing machine.'

'I can handle him. I'm a good rider. I know what I'm doing.'

'Yes. I said almost the same thing, word for word, to that cop. We *may* think we're indestructible but—'

'Mario, don't do this. I don't want to end the afternoon with an argument when I know I won't be seeing you for nearly a week.'

'But that's where you're wrong. I think it's time we gave Mrs Mackintosh more than your virtue to think about. We're going to visit an antique jeweller I know in Bourke Street. I think it's high time we made it official and bought you a ring.'

'A ring?' She was suddenly still, unsure whether to take him seriously or not. 'That's a big step. Considering I have to share you with somebody else.'

'What are you talking about?' He looked astounded. 'You know there's nobody else in my life.'

'Isn't there?' she whispered. On the one hand she was tempted to accept his declaration at face value but there was still that niggling doubt about the photograph he kept on his bedside table. He might get angry and secretive again but she couldn't pretend the photograph didn't exist. So she took a deep breath and asked.

'Who is the girl in the photograph you keep by your bed?'

His expression clouded and his shoulders slumped but this time he answered her. 'That is my cousin Rina. She died.'

'Your cousin? Oh Mario, I'm so sorry.' Corey had no cousins of her own but she did know they could be close as brother and sister. 'How did it—?'

'It shouldn't have happened.' He cut short her question. 'I don't like to talk about it.'

'No. No, of course not.' Corey said, blaming herself for putting a damper on the afternoon. 'I suppose you were close.'

He nodded and Corey knew that, for now, she would get nothing more from him.

He started the motor, made sure the anchor was safely aboard and set off for the shore.

# CHAPTER EIGHT

THE jewellery shop was housed in an ornate Victorian building – yet another museum in Corey's opinion. She found it daunting at first with its high, vaulted ceilings and rooms full of tall showcases filled with priceless antique jewels, until a cheerful sales assistant put her at ease; a girl not much older than herself.

'You have small hands – dainty hands – although you put them to practical use,' she said, turning Corey's hands in her own to look at them, remarking on the square-cut, unvarnished nails. 'And I see you're not one for nail enamel and other time-consuming vanities.' She looked up for confirmation, smiling as Corey gave it with a nod. 'So perhaps something simple would be more appropriate—'

'Nothing so simple that it looks mean,' Mario interrupted, pointing out an ornate Victorian cluster – a huge diamond surrounded by rubies, perhaps the most flamboyant and expensive piece on the tray. 'How about this one?'

'Oh, Mario—' Corey started shaking her head.

'Go on. Try it – just to please me.'

Corey put it on but apart from being several sizes too large, the ring looked clumsy, like a knuckle-duster on her small hand. 'It *is* beautiful,' Corey murmured tactfully. 'But I'm not sure I should have rubies at all. Aren't they supposed to be forty years down the track?'

The sales assistant nodded and produced another tray of more modest jewels, most of which Mario rejected as being too ordinary. But the girl, who was a clever saleswoman, conspired with Corey to divert him to a single square cut emerald set in platinum with a small diamond on either side. In the end they almost had him convinced he had chosen it himself.

'It's perfect, sir,' the saleswoman enthused. 'And so suitable for the young lady's hand.' She moved Corey's finger so that it sparkled under the lights. 'This jewel was crafted in England some time in the nineteen thirties, so it's a vintage piece rather than strictly antique.'

Delighted with their choice, they went to celebrate in the bar of a fashionable hotel at the top of Collins Street. Corey had been there before but only for racing events. All the same she was recognized by a gossip columnist accompanied by a cameraman who lost no time in taking some pictures and making notes.

'And are you also involved in the racing industry Mr – er—?' the girl asked, pointing her dictaphone towards Mario and waiting for him to give his name.

'Antonello – Mario Antonello,' he said dismissively, irritated by the reporter's intrusion into their private celebration.

161

'Not connected to Antonello Fashions, I suppose?' The girl said, expecting him to deny it. Mario hesitated, clearly tempted to do so.

' 'Fraid so. My father is Guido Antonello the CEO, presently on holiday in Europe.'

'Wonderful!' the girl gushed. 'I get two celebrities for the price of one. If these pictures are any good, we could make the front page.'

'Of the paper?' Mario frowned.

'No – they keep that for disasters and terror attack. The front page of the Sunday magazine. Now if you could just give me a bit more background—'

'Not now, thanks,' Mario cut her short. 'We're trying to celebrate our engagement.'

'I know and I'm sorry.' The girl was persistent and didn't sound sorry at all. 'But I can't let it go at that. Our readers will be agog to know how the fashion house met up with the promising girl jockey. Was it at one of the racing carnivals? Fashions on the Field?'

'I'm associated with the trainer, Tony Mackintosh,' Corey was more willing to give information than Mario. 'He put me on Mario's horse, Pirate King.'

'So it's a real racing romance,' the girl almost cooed. 'That could be my headline for the article.'

'No article, thanks.' Mario scowled. 'A brief announcement will be quite enough. As I said before – we're trying to have a private celebration here.'

'Oh, OK. I know when I'm being given the brush-off.' The girl pouted, realizing she would get nothing more. Her photographer jogged her arm, pointing out a television talk show host about to be seated with his entourage and they took off at speed, weaving their way between the tables to get to him before anyone else.

Having been the subject of the reporter's interest, Corey and Mario were still attracting attention so they left, deciding not to lunch at the hotel after all. Instead, they collected some Chinese take-away and prawn crackers from the food court to reheat at home.

Seated at Mario's enormous kitchen table, they were still eating their meal when the telephone rang. Mario was about to leave the machine to answer it until he recognized the voice of his mother, calling from Rome. This was something she rarely did when she was away and, in Europe, it would still be the middle of the previous night. He picked it up quickly.

'Mama? Yes Mama, I'm here.' Corey noticed his tone soften as he spoke to his mother. He was clearly very fond of her. 'What's up?'

'Oh Mario, I hate those machines. I never know if you're really there or not.'

'It *is* me, Mama. I'm here at home having lunch.'

'Isn't that marvellous? Over here it's still night.'

'Mama, what is it? I'm sure you didn't call to chat about the time difference. Is anything wrong?'

'*Sí, sí*. It's your papa. He's been very sick.'

'Not a heart attack?' This was something Mario had been expecting for some time. His father was one of those men who could never relax. Although he was supposed to be on holiday when he visited Italy, it was impossible for him not to meddle in the day to day business of Antonello

163

Enterprises in Rome. The proposed shipping line was especially dear to his heart.

Realizing from Mario's tone and expression that there was bad news, Corey also stopped eating and set down her chopsticks.

'Not a heart attack but still bad,' his mother went on to say. 'He has had a small stroke – no, not severe – but a warning that he should slow down and take better care of himself.'

'I've been telling him that for two years. So how is he now? Is he getting good care?'

'*Sí, sí.* Out of hospital now. But here he seems to see a new doctor each day – he doesn't like that when he's feeling confused. He wants his own doctor at home to take care of him – Doctor Milano in Melbourne.'

'But is he well enough to travel? It won't be too much of a strain?'

'You know your father – so stubborn – even when he's sick. To try and stop him when he's determined, will only make him worse. If the doctors say he's well enough to travel, he will.'

'Well, keep me posted.'

'Oh and by the way,' his mother went on. 'Isabella has rescued your little girlfriend in Paris. Dominic recovered her plane ticket as well. You'll be seeing her soon, I'm sure. A sweet girl, Isabella says.'

'No Mama, you have it all wrong. Maeve's not a girlfriend – I don't even know her. I am seeing her sister, Corey.'

'Her sister? That sounds complicated.'

'Well, it's not. And while we're talking I have some news for you, too. As of today, Corey and I are engaged.' He looked across at Corey and smiled as he said this.

'Cora? I don't know any Cora. Who is she? This is all very sudden, Mario. It's not like you, to be so – impulsive. Before we leave, you don't even have one girl friend. Now it seems you have two.'

'Mama, listen to me. I don't have two girlfriends.' Exasperated, he raised his eyes heavenwards, then glanced at Corey, shaking his head. 'I'll explain it all later, when you get back. Give Papa my love and tell him not to worry – I'm on top of everything here. And if you're thinking of coming home soon, break the journey in Singapore – it will be less of a strain. Keep in touch and let me know your flight number as soon as you have it. I'll come and meet you.'

He came off the phone and told Corey the good news about Maeve, followed by the less happy news of his father.

'But he'll get better? He is going to be OK?' She said, biting her lip. She knew from experience how quickly illness could take hold, robbing people of beloved parents.

Mario shrugged. 'We can but hope. He expects too much of himself – forgets he is old. Telling him to slow down is like telling the tide not to turn.'

After her initial relief that they had not appeared on the cover of the Sunday magazine – that privilege being reserved for a television presenter – Corey turned the page to reveal a photograph of Mario scowling at the camera while she appeared as no more than a blur in the background. The caption read 'From Two Different Worlds' and the paragraph beneath contained nothing but unfair comparisons and speculation as to how long the engagement might last.

Looking at it, Corey felt all her old doubts and insecurities surface yet again. They *were* from different worlds and, even with Mario's ring on her finger, from time to time she still wondered what he saw in her. The conversation with Pat hadn't helped. She had been quick to point out that Mario came from a world of high fashion, wealth and privilege. He lived in a Toorak mansion while she was no more than a farmer's daughter from the bush. Even now, after so many passionate encounters, so many promises and declarations of love, there were still times when she felt that she didn't really belong.

She twisted her engagement ring, thinking of it as a talisman – a defence against a cruel and envious world. She reminded herself that no one had forced Mario to make any promises or declarations – he had chosen to do so of his own accord. She hadn't even been thinking of marriage until Pat raised the subject. She tore the magazine in half and threw it in the bin for recycling, comforting herself with the thought that many people didn't bother to read newspapers at the weekend. She decided not to mention it to Mario – with any luck he might not have seen it.

As it turned out, it was Maeve who returned home before Mario's parents. Corey drove to the city to meet her, wondering about her sister's plans for the future. Clearly, her marriage to Jon Manolito was over and, without an income, she would have to find work at once to provide for her own future.

When she caught sight of Corey standing patiently waiting for her as she came through from Customs, Maeve dropped her solitary bag to the floor, flung her arms around her sister's neck and burst into tears. It was several minutes before she could speak but eventually, she stopped crying, blew her nose loudly and managed a watery smile.

'Sorry about that,' she said. 'I'm OK really. These are tears of relief. I'm so happy to see you – to be back home. For a while there, I didn't think I was going to make it.'

'It's all right,' Corey hugged her again. 'You've had a rough time.'

Maeve shuddered theatrically. 'You don't know the half of it. I was ready to jump in the Seine until Isabella turned up. She and her husband were wonderful. And I feel so guilty when I remember the lies Jon told me about that family.'

'Not your fault.'

'Lets get out of here, shall we?. I've seen enough of airports to last me a lifetime.'

'Where to, then?' Corey said as they joined the stream of traffic on the Tullamarine freeway. 'You know you're welcome to come and stay with me for a while.'

'Thanks but no thanks,' Maeve smiled. Once her initial storm of weeping was over, she seemed much more together than Corey expected. 'I'd only be in your way.'

'I wouldn't mind,' Corey murmured although she was secretly relieved. For some reason she couldn't fathom, Maeve had never been a favourite with Pat and Maeve, in turn, had always been jealous of Pat's place in Corey's affections. 'If you feel you need more time to get yourself together—'

'Thanks, Sis, but I've wasted enough time already. I need to get on with the rest of my life.'

'Where are we going, then? Not back to your old flat?'

'Only for a night or two. I need to pack up my things and grab some clothes. I'll send anything saleable to the auction rooms – the bastard owes me that much at least. That exotic home theatre system of his should fetch a few dollars. Then I'll drop off the keys to the agents so they can re-let the flat.'

'Leaving you homeless. Then what?'

'I didn't get much sleep on the plane so I had plenty of time to think and make plans. D'you remember my best friend, Susie, from college?'

'Yes, I do,' Corey smiled, remembering a large, cheerful girl with an infectious giggle. She and Maeve had been inseparable. 'I haven't seen her for ages.'

'Neither have I. Because she's running her own model agency up on the Gold Coast. Every time we talk she asks me to join her – she wants someone to help her expand the business but it has to be someone she trusts.'

'Sounds like a great idea – if the offer's still open.'

'It will be. She says she'd rather soldier on alone than take anyone else.'

'And what about Jon? Are you certain he won't be back?'

'Not he. His cover's well and truly blown. The final straw was when Astrid told me I'm probably not even his wife. She thinks he's still married to someone in England – never bothered to get a divorce.'

Corey considered this for a moment, remembering Jon's flippant remarks about marriage as well as his unwelcome advances on their wedding day. Maeve was well rid of him; an irresponsible philanderer who used everyone and didn't care who got hurt along the way. 'So where does that leave you?'

'Free. If I'm not married to Jon, I can't be held responsible for the failure of his business or his debts. And if he is stupid enough to come back, he could face a charge of bigamy.'

'Right.' Corey didn't say more. She could only hope everything would be resolved as easily as Maeve hoped. Although her sister was doing her best to put a brave face on it, she must be devastated by Jon's many betrayals and the collapse of her marriage.

'My, that's a pretty ring.' Satisfied for now that her own life was back on course, Maeve had caught sight of Corey's newly decorated hand on the steering wheel, the ring glinting in the sunlight. 'Been buying ourselves expensive presents, have we?'

'Not exactly.' Corey said slowly. She had been reluctant to speak of her own happiness when life had been treating her sister so badly.

'That's never a real emerald?'

'Look again.' Corey smiled, keeping her eyes on the road ahead.

'It is.' Maeve peered at it more closely. 'An engagement ring! But Corey – surely not – it can't be—?'

Corey nodded. ' 'Fraid so.'

'Well, why didn't you say so before? Oh, darling, that's

wonderful news.' Impulsively, Maeve wrapped an arm round her neck and hugged her. 'And I love that ring – it's just beautiful.'

'Careful!' Corey almost swerved on to the hard shoulder. 'You'll have us both in the ditch.'

'I thought about it after you called and wondered what Mr Antonello was doing at your place at that time of night.' Maeve was silent for a moment, thinking. 'But, Sis, are you sure about this? It's all a bit sudden, isn't it? You haven't known him more than a couple of months.'

'How long does it take to fall in love?'

'No time at all.' Maeve gave in with a smile. 'OK. I suppose I'm unduly cautious after my experiences with Jon.'

'Well, he's gone from your life forever and you're not to let him cast a shadow over your future.'

'I won't,' Maeve spoke up bravely although Corey knew it would be some time before her sister would trust enough to give her heart again.

After leaving Maeve at her flat to call her old friend and sort out her plans for the future, Corey should have gone back to the coast but decided on impulse to go and see Mario instead.

As she parked her car outside those forbidding iron gates, it was brought home to her yet again how different his lifestyle was from her own. He didn't live in a suburban house where she could just turn up and knock on the door. Instead she had to ring the bell at the gate like a medieval traveller until he decided to let her in. A glance at her watch told her it was still early, not even 7 a.m. Just as she was about to drive off again without disturbing him, the gates opened and, as she drove in, Mario appeared at the door, unshaven and wearing a dark red bath robe. He was scrubbing his hands through his hair to wake himself and as she stepped out of the car and walked towards him, his face broke into a slow, welcoming smile, making her heart lurch.

He gathered her into his warm arms and rested his chin on her head. 'This a nice surprise. You look fresh as the morning and just what I wanted for breakfast. Come back to bed with me while it's still warm.'

'I'd love to, Mario, but I really do have to get home. Tony's expecting me.'

'Tony's always expecting you,' he grumbled, pulling her inside before she could change her mind and closing the door behind her. 'So what brings you to the city today?'

'I just collected my sister from the airport.'

'Yeah? How is she?'

'Better than I expected. She's gone to clear out the flat and give the keys back to the agents.' Briefly, she gave him an outline of Maeve's plans.

'I hope it works out for her. She deserves a break after the rough time she had with Manolito.'

'She'll be OK. We're made of stern stuff, we O'Briens.'

'As I'm discovering, sometimes to my cost.' He started walking towards the kitchen. 'Coffee?'

'Please. Any news of your father?'

'Coming home some time this week. My mother says he's a terrible patient.' On reaching the kitchen, he opened cupboards and busied himself making coffee while Corey set out the cups. 'Do you want breakfast?'

'I brought it for you.' She handed him a paper bag. 'Croissants from the French bakery – still warm.'

'A woman after my own heart,' he said, heading for the stairs. 'Keep an eye on that coffee. I'm going to clean my teeth and then I can kiss you properly.'

'Oh, Mario, I really don't—'

'Have time?' He grinned wickedly. 'We'll see about that. Waking a bloke in the middle of the night should incur some sort of penalty.'

'It's hardly the middle of the night,' she protested, laughing. 'I'm usually out with the horses long before six. Even builders start work at seven a.m. on the dot.'

'But I'm not a builder,' he said, galloping up the stairs two at a time. 'Pour the coffee and bring the croissants with you when you come up.'

'I'm not coming up,' she called after him. 'If there's anything I hate it is crumbs in the bed.'

'You didn't seem to mind them at your place,' he said, looking over the banister.

He returned in less than five minutes, still unshaven but smelling of mint and wearing a navy tracksuit. His normally springy hair, fresh from the shower, lay in wet curls close to his head. He accepted the coffee she gave him and studied her thoughtfully.

'You don't really like this house, do you?' he said, coming straight to the point. He was intuitive enough to know that it wasn't just crumbs that were keeping her from his bedroom upstairs.

She bit her lips and avoided his gaze, unsure what to say.

'It's OK – I'm not offended. Because you're quite right – it *is* a museum. I bought it for Anna because I thought she wanted a showpiece.' He took a sip of his coffee and sighed. 'As it turned out, she didn't like it much either.'

'I'm sorry.'

'Sorry about Anna or sorry that you don't like it?'

'Both.'

'So what do you want me to do? Sell it and buy something smaller? Or would you be happier in a ranch-style house in the country where you can have horses?'

'I don't know, Mario. Our engagement – everything – it's all so new. But you can't change everything in your life just for me.'

'Why not? Lets put our cards on the table here. When we're married, I'll expect you to change some of the things about *your* life to suit me.'

'Such as?' She was suddenly wary.

Intuitively, he caught on to her change of mood. 'Don't worry about it. I have one or two ideas but we don't need to thrash out the details right now.'

'I'm sorry but I think we do. If this is another ploy to stop me from riding professionally—'

'Did I say anything about riding? I don't think so.'

'Well, you wouldn't, would you? The changes are happening so gradually, you think I won't notice. Tony's already talking to Ray Mercer about Pirate King. On your instructions, I hear.'

'Why not? Pirate was Ray's ride long before he was yours. And you're still suspended, remember.'

'Not for long. Only one more week and I shall be back in the saddle.'

173

'Don't remind me,' he shot back and took a large bite of his croissant, munching angrily.

Corey was silent for a moment, staring at her hand lying flat on the table and the lovely engagement ring that had been on her finger for scarcely a week. Everyone seemed to think it was all too sudden – Maeve, Pat, even Mario's mother – and maybe it was. On impulse, she started to twist it off until Mario stopped her, pushing it back into place and kissing her hand.

'Corey, don't throw out the baby with the bath water,' he said softly. 'I know we have things to work through. That item in the newspaper must have upset you – I wasn't too happy about it myself. But we're not going to let them get the better of us, are we? Least of all prove them right.'

Seeing the tears gathering in her eyes, he pulled her into his arms and kissed her with tenderness rather than passion this time. She snuggled close, letting her head rest on his shoulder and breathing in the warm, masculine smell of him. When she was with him, like this, everything seemed all right. It was only when they were apart that the doubts came creeping in.

'My parents will be home soon,' he whispered, hugging her even closer. 'I want you to meet them. My mother is the kindest person in the world and I know she's going to love you.'

Corey could only hope that was true. But at the same time she knew it was going to be hard for Julia Antonello to part with her only son to a woman who was better at riding a racehorse than striding a catwalk, wearing high fashion. She couldn't even bake a decent lasagne.

*

All her doubts returned in full measure as they stood on the doorstep of the pristine modern villa that Mario's parents called home. It stood on high ground, designed to make the most of a beautiful view of the river, the city beyond. Even the tiny garden was carefully landscaped, the bedding plants standing to attention like soldiers, the lawn recently mown and the edges severely clipped. No weed would be allowed to flourish here. Would she?

'I'm not sure I should have come,' she whispered. 'You father's been ill – and I'm sure they'd rather see you alone. Maybe I should wait until he's better.'

'So you can stress on it and get more nervous than ever?' He put an arm round her shoulders and gave her a squeeze. 'Relax and just be yourself. My mother will love you. She has the biggest heart in the world—'

'And your father? I'm sure he has greater ambitions for his son than to marry a stable girl—'

'I'm sure he'll find you very stable and sensible.' He dropped a kiss on her head.

'That's not what I mean and you know it,' she hissed. But there was no time to say anything more. The door was flung wide and a woman nearly as tall as Mario himself swept him into her embrace. Neatly coiffed and discreetly made-up, Julia Antonello was handsome rather than beautiful, an elegant woman perhaps in her early sixties.

'It's so good to see you.' At first she had no eyes for anyone but her son. She kissed him soundly on both cheeks and held his face in her hands. 'Looking well, too – not so haunted for once.'

'Mama.' He extricated himself and drew Corey into their circle. 'Mama, this is Corey the girl I told you about. We are going to be married.'

At last Mrs Antonello turned her attention to the girl who was standing beside him, waiting to be introduced. It was there for only a second and she recovered quickly but momentarily Corey saw shock and surprise in the older woman's eyes before she too was embraced with a formal kiss on both cheeks. Julia smelled of an expensive yet subtle floral perfume and her sweater was obviously cashmere.

'Sweet girl,' she murmured, giving Corey a speculative look. 'How long have you known my son?'

'Later, Mama.' Mario moved forward, drawing Corey with him. 'You'll have plenty of time to quiz her later on. But how is Papa, really? Tell me the truth.'

His mother shrugged. 'I don't know. Doctor Milano says he's making good progress but Guido doesn't believe him. Some days are better than others.'

'But he is going to get well? He'll recover completely in time?'

Once more his mother shrugged. 'Too early to say.' She ushered them into a cosy sitting room, a real log fire blazing in the hearth, filling the room with the strong eucalypt scent of the Australian bush. 'Sit down both of you and I'll get him up. He wanted me to rouse him just as soon as you arrived.'

'I could go and see him in bed?' Mario offered.

'No.' Julia shook her head. 'He is impatient with his

weakness and refuses to stay in bed more than an hour or so at a time.'

Corey turned to Mario as soon as his mother left the room. 'I knew I shouldn't have come,' she said. 'Your mother's quite stressed. This introduction could have waited until a more suitable time.'

'Giving you time to get even colder feet?' He took her hand and kissed it, turning her hand to admire the ring. 'We were right about the emerald – it does suit your hand.'

They both sprang to their feet as the door opened, Guido Antonello's querulous voice preceding him. 'Don't fuss, Julia.' He moved slowly into the room, pushing his wife's gentle hands away. 'I'm all right.'

Mario was shocked by his father's appearance and had to work hard not to show it. Since the stroke, the old man had aged ten years. Where he had always been upright before with an almost military briskness and bearing, one shoulder had dropped and he now had to walk with the aid of a stick. It was hard to believe the stroke had been mild.

Before, when Mario met his father after a time apart, their greetings had been exuberant bear hugs. This time, conscious of the old man's fragile appearance, he embraced him gently with a kiss on both cheeks.

But it wasn't Mario who engaged Guido's attention but Corey. He shuffled towards her, blinking and peering at her as if he couldn't believe his eyes.

'Rina?' he whispered. 'Rina, is that really you? Come back to us after all this time?'

'Papa!' Julia spoke sharply, plucking at his sleeve. 'What are you thinking of? Of course that's not Rina – it's Corey.

Mario's new fiancée – the girl I told you about—'

But the old man went on as if he didn't hear her. '*Sì, sì!* Rina.'

'I'm so sorry,' Julia whispered to Corey. 'You can see he's not well. Confusing the past with the present. Wandering in his mind.' She turned to her husband. 'Now, Papa. Sit down there and don't move.' She assisted him into an armchair and put a footstool under his feet. 'I'm going to bring us some coffee and some of my special biscuits. Unless,' she said to Corey, 'you'd rather have tea?'

'Excuse me?' Staring at Mario's father and trying to make sense of his words, she hadn't heard anything Julia said.

'Would you rather have tea?'

'No, not at all.' Corey murmured, doubting if she would be able to swallow anything. 'Coffee's fine.' She glanced at Mario who had his hand over his mouth and was staring at his father as if he were a bomb about to explode.

'But – Rina. How is it that she is alive?' The old man was speaking his thoughts aloud. 'I thought she died. I'm sure she did. We went to the funeral—'

'Papa, don't stress yourself, please.' Mario's voice was an urgent whisper. 'This can't be good for you.'

'It's no good – I don't remember.' The old man sighed, shaking his head. 'So much I can't remember.'

Fortunately, at that moment, Julia reappeared with the coffee and Corey sprang up, offering help, grateful to have something to do.

Although it cost him a great deal of effort, Mario's father managed to eat and drink, spilling only a small amount of coffee into his saucer. Julia chattered on, making sure there were no awkward silences. She questioned Corey about her work, seeming genuinely interested in her answers.

'Is marvellous. These days you girls, you can do anything – anything you want. For me was only to work in a shop or an office until I get married.' She laughed and glanced at her son. 'You should be proud of Corey – encourage her – she is very smart girl.' She saw Mario lift his shoulders in a shrug. 'And wassamatter with you today? Cat got your tongue?'

*Signora,*' Corey began. 'I should very much like to see—'

'Call me Julia please,' the older woman interrupted, pulling a face. '*Signora* always makes me feel so old, like my mother.'

'Julia—' Corey persisted. She knew Mario wouldn't like what she was about to say but she was going for it, anyway. This may be her only chance. 'Do you have any photos of Mario's cousin Rina – I should so like to see—'

'Oh, I don't know,' Julia frowned. 'When we moved to this smaller house, so much had to go.'

'And we should be going, too.' Mario sprang to his feet, taking that as a cue. 'We don't want Papa to get over-tired.'

'How can I get tired? Lying on my back all day?' The old man smiled. 'The album, Julia. It's in the desk.' Impatiently, he poked his stick in that direction. 'There are pictures of Rina.'

Reluctantly, Julia went to the desk and drew out a leather bound album. 'We may not have any left.' She flicked through some of the pages. 'I might have given them all to her mother.'

'Please.' Corey held out her hand for it, leaving Julia no

179

option but to pass it across. 'This is part of your family history and I'd like to see it anyway.'

Inside were the early photographs, common to any family album. Victorian Italians, stiffly posed for the camera, wearing their Sunday best, high-collared shirts and wide taffeta gowns. Then came more black and white snapshots taken by amateurs, mostly of children and pets, making Corey wonder if she was ever going to find what she was looking for. She moved on, flicking through colour photographs taken from the fifties to the eighties, allowing Julia to point out Mario as a baby.

Mario started to pace the room, tense as a caged lion. His father, lying back in his armchair had fallen asleep and was snoring gently.

Suddenly, Corey found what she was looking for – a studio portrait of a girl on a horse – both groomed in readiness for a major equestrian event. She blinked, scarcely able to believe her eyes. Were it not for the longer, much fairer hair caught back in a snood, it might have been a photograph of herself. This girl was more like her than Maeve. There were snapshots, too, of the same girl laughing up at Mario and, most telling of all, with their arms around each other, sitting on the beach. There was also another which she now recognized as the portrait Mario kept by his bed in a silver frame. Taking her time, she studied all these pictures again before quietly closing the album and handing it back to Julia.

'Thank you,' she said in a small voice. 'I think that tells me all that I need to know.' She rose to her feet and glanced at and through Mario. All she wanted now was to leave with her dignity, without breaking down.

'Corey,' he said brokenly, taking a step towards her. 'This is not what you think.'

She didn't answer him, speaking softly to his mother so as not to rouse the old man who was sound asleep. 'Thanks for the hospitality, Mrs Antonello, it was very enlightening. I don't suppose we'll be seeing each other again.' She fumbled in her bag for her cell phone as she made her way unsteadily towards the door. 'Stay with your parents, Mario. I'll call a cab.'

Julia still clutching the album, sat there shocked and silent with tears standing in her eyes although, for the moment, Corey's own eyes were dry. Mario, followed her to the door, trying to talk to her.

'Corey, wait. At least give me a chance to explain.'

But she was already outside, giving directions to the cab company on her phone.

'Explain what, Mario?' She clicked off the phone, trying to hold herself together and keep her voice steady. 'That I was never more than a substitute for your Rina?. How stupid I was to believe that you loved and wanted to marry *me*.'

'I *do* love you, Corey. You have to believe that. I'm sure we could be—'

'Happy together? I don't think so, not now. Not now your secret is out.'

'You're so wrong about everything. You don't under-stand.'

'I do. You told me a half-truth – so much better than an outright lie. You let me think you loved your cousin as a sister. But it wasn't like that at all, was it? You were lovers.'

'Not really. Not like you and I. She was far too shy and retiring to—'

'Make herself as available to you as I did?'

'It was years ago, Corey. Times were different. We were both so young.'

'Why didn't you tell me the truth from the start? Did you honestly think you could introduce me to your family, maybe even marry me and expect me not to find out? That I was never more to you than a copy? A pale substitute for the woman you really loved?' Seeing she had shocked him into silence, she pressed home her advantage, tugging off her engagement ring and forcing it into his hand. 'Take this ring and keep it with that photograph. I'm sure it belongs to Rina far more than it ever belonged to me.'

At this moment, her cab arrived outside the front gate and the driver got out to open the door for her. Before Mario could say anything further, she sprang into the back seat, signalling to the driver that she was ready to leave. She didn't look back but somehow she sensed that Mario was standing in the road behind them, watching the cab as it pulled away. It was only as she was giving directions to Mario's house to pick up her car that she remembered it was standing in the driveway behind those tall iron gates. She wouldn't be able to leave until Mario came home.

She paid off the cab driver and sat down under a tree to wait. Just as she thought she would have to swallow her pride and call him, she heard the distinctive sound of Mario's Ferrari, tyres complaining as he negotiated the bumps and curves of these quiet streets. She stood up, waiting in silence while he unlocked the gates and followed him as he drove inside. He parked his car beside hers and climbed out, striding purposefully towards her.

'Please don't say anything,' she muttered, scarcely able to look at him. 'I just want to go home.'

'Corey, you're upset. You shouldn't be driving while you're in this mood.'

She did look at him then. 'My moods are no longer any concern of yours.'

'That so?' His blue eyes seemed to shoot sparks as he took refuge in anger. 'Guilty as charged, am I? To be hanged, drawn and quartered without the benefit of a trial?'

'Mario, please. Don't make this harder than it needs to be.'

'Corey.' He tried to take her by the shoulders but she shrugged his hands away. 'What do I have to do? What can I possibly say to make things right between us?'

'Nothing.' She stared at the stones on the driveway. 'It's too late for that.'

'It doesn't have to be. OK I was wrong. I should have told you the whole truth about Rina from the beginning. But how would it have sounded? *I'm falling in love with you because you look like the cousin I loved and lost?*'

She raised her eyes to look at him then, slowly shaking her head. For just a moment, he thought she was weakening.

'You don't really look like Rina. It's only a first impression.'

'It impressed your parents well enough.' Immediately,

she was back on the defensive. 'She's more like me than Maeve. She could be my twin sister.'

'We were just kids. And it was all so long ago—'

'Don't try to explain it away as calf love. It was much more than that. It ruined your marriage to Anna.'

'That was doomed from the start. It should never have happened.'

'But the fact is that it did and I'm afraid the same thing could happen to us. History has an unpleasant habit of repeating itself.'

'So you won't even take the risk? Give me one more chance?'

'You lied to me, Mario,' she said softly. 'If only by omission. We can't build a future together, founded on lies.' Carefully, she walked around him on her way to her car, moving stealthily as a cat in fear of being chased. Defeated now, he made no move to stand in her way. To her relief, the car started obediently and she drove in a wide circle to avoid reversing so that she could accelerate when she reached the road.

As she drove slowly home, she thought about what she would say to Tony and Pat. As little as possible, she decided at last. Fortunately, she had never made much of her engagement, never wearing her ring when she was riding or working around the stables. With any luck they might not realize it was gone.

Mario closed the gates behind her, trudged up the driveway and let himself into the gloomy, empty house. He had a lot to think about.

Before he left his parents' house, his mother had told him

some uncomfortable home truths.

'I know this isn't a good time for you, Mario, but there are some important matters we need to discuss—'

'Can't it wait, Mama? I have to catch up with Corey – see if there's a chance I can put things right.'

'Let her go, Mario.' Julia's tone was gentle if determined. 'She is hurting too much to think clearly now. Leave her and in time she may see things differently. You must let fate decide.'

'Fate!'

'Yes. If you are meant to be together, you will.' She smiled, shaking her head. 'You are so like your father. One day you will find out you can't control everything in your life.'

'But—'

'Mario, listen to me. You can see how your father is – too sick for work any more. I know you have these other interests – your racing connections. But the time has come for you to give up these – diversions.'

'They're much more than diversions. I'm committed to Tony and Pat. I won't let them down.'

'So? You prefer to let us down instead?' his mother said softly, her eyes full of sadness. 'I know your father's retirement has come much earlier than we expected and it is a shock. But you have to devote yourself to the family business.'

'Mama, you worry too much. The business runs smoothly enough and we have excellent staff.'

'It isn't the same as family,' she said with a stubborn twist to the lips. 'You should know what is going on at all times.'

185

'I do. Business isn't as ponderous, these days. A CEO doesn't have to spend all day in the office. We deal with things faster through phone calls and emails.'

'Machines! I don't trust machines.' Julia frowned. 'The business needs *you* Mario and your undivided attention. Is it so much to ask? For your father's peace of mind?'

It was. It was asking him to shelve his horse breeding programme and all his plans for the future. Ignoring his mother's advice, he had left his parents' house, intent on salvaging his relationship with Corey. He hadn't succeeded in that, either. He shivered, trapped by the responsibilities his mother had heaped on him and also desperately lonely in that cold, deserted museum of a house.

# CHAPTER NINE

C orey was agreeably surprised. Returning to the track after her suspension, she found herself suddenly in demand. In addition to riding for Tony, she accepted a full card for a local country meeting and the following week had several bookings for Flemington in the city. These were the races leading up to the Spring Carnival and, if she could convert at least some of these rides into winners, she would be in the frame to compete in some of the major events at that time.

She avoided Mario when he came to the stables and for once was grateful that Tony had engaged Ray Mercer to ride Pirate. Setting aside all thoughts of a personal life, she threw herself wholeheartedly into her work. If her thoughts did stray towards Mario, she would banish them, repeating to herself like a mantra – *He never loved you, never – you have to forget.*

Only Pat was brave enough to bring up the subject of her missing engagement ring as they chatted over coffee when she came back from exercising the horses one morning.

Since breaking it off with Mario, Corey had avoided such cosy chats but on this wintry July day, the freshly brewed coffee smelled wonderful, too good to refuse.

Without preamble Pat came straight to the point. 'That was the shortest engagement I've ever seen. What happened?'

Corey stared out of Pat's kitchen window, pretending to focus on the horizon as she fought the familiar tightness forming at the back of her throat. 'I can't talk about it,' she murmured. 'Not yet.'

'I think you should try,' Pat said gently. 'It doesn't help to bottle things up.'

'He doesn't love me, that's all,' Corey blurted. 'Never did.'

'Are you sure?' Pat sat back, regarding her. 'If all he wanted was a casual relationship, why would he ask you to marry him? Or go to the trouble of buying a ring?'

'Why, indeed,' Corey said, not without bitterness.

'And he introduced you to his family. He is Italian, you know they don't do these things lightly.'

'Meeting his family.' Corey took a shuddering breath, remembering. 'That's what brought everything to a head.'

'They didn't approve?'

'I wish it were that simple.' Corey glanced at her watch and stood up. 'Thanks for the coffee, Pat. But I really do have to go. I've a full card today and I mustn't be late.'

'There's plenty of time. And you haven't even tasted that coffee. Corey, sit down. I mean to get to the bottom of this. When Mario started showing an interest in you, I was afraid you'd be the one to get hurt. Now I'm much more worried about *him*. Have you seen him lately?'

'No,' she said in a small voice. 'I've been keeping out of his way.'

'I've never seen such a change in anyone. He was always so well turned out but now his clothes are crumpled as if he's been sleeping in them. He doesn't seem to care about anything and sometimes can't even be bothered to shave. I don't think he eats unless I set food right in front of him and that haunted look has come back – even worse than before. There are dark circles under his eyes as if he's getting no sleep.'

Uncomfortably, Corey shrugged. 'His father's not well. Maybe it's that.'

'No, Corey, it's more. The man is in torment. Something's eating at him from within.'

'Well, what can I do about it?' Corey was immediately on the defensive. 'None of this is my fault.' Right now she would have liked to give way and cry on Pat's shoulder, telling the whole sorry tale, but pride wouldn't allow it. At present, the only way she could hold herself together was by pretending that Mario Antonello didn't exist.

'All right.' Pat held up her hands in surrender. 'It's your life and I won't interfere. But when I see the pair of you making each other miserable, separated by some stupid misunderstanding, it just breaks my heart.'

'I told you, Pat – it's much more than a lovers' tiff. Now I really do have to be going.' And she ran from the room before Pat could say anything else.

At the country race meeting that afternoon, she seemed unstoppable – luck and opportunity seemed to be going

189

her way. Although from time to time Pat's words kept coming back to haunt her – *The man is in torment. Something's eating at him from within* – she managed to keep her mind on the job. She rode two winners in succession and the racegoers loved it, singing *Corey! Corey!* and applauding her as she rode back to scale. Normally, she would have been thrilled but, although she smiled and acknowledged the tribute, she could take no real pleasure in it.

Her ride was scratched in the fourth race and with two winners in her pocket already, she was happy to sit this one out and watch Ray Mercer ride Pirate King. Leaning on the fence, she was watching the strappers lead the horses into the mounting yard when Tony came flying across the lawn towards her.

'Corey, thank God you're still here. Ray's in trouble – can't make the weight. You'll have to ride Pirate King.'

'Tony, I can't. You know Mario doesn't want me anywhere near him.'

'To hell with what Mario wants – there's no time. Less than fifteen minutes before the race. You'll have to ride him or I'll have to scratch.'

'OK,' she said, grabbing the silks from Tony and racing to get changed

If her luck held and she could make Pirate win, Mario would have to eat his words and admit she could handle him.

Mario had discovered his mother was right. Now that everyone in the company knew that Guido Antonello was out of action for good, they expected his son to take over, making all the decisions and giving advice. It was far too much for one person and something would have to go but he was determined not to abandon his racing interests. The shipping line maybe? That was still up in the air, the deal never finalized. And in the long term, if not in his parents' lifetime, he might sell off their business interests in Italy. But right now, it was a question of keeping all the plates spinning and this kept him busy, well into the evening each day.

Nobody knew, not even his parents, that he had sold his mansion in Toorak. It had been snapped up with surprising speed even before it came on the open market. He hadn't realized the property would be in such high demand.

From the same agents, he purchased a country property at Mount Macedon – having stables and paddocks attached to a well-maintained farmhouse built of local stone. It seemed an ideal location; a country area but still within easy reach of the city, giving him the best of both worlds. He saw it as an extension of the business he already shared with Tony and Pat. Here his dream of breeding horses would become a reality. His imported mares would thrive in the clear mountain air of Mount Macedon, raising healthy foals until they were old enough to be sold or transferred to Tony at Mornington. He had looked at many properties before settling on this one, knowing that Corey would share his dream, falling in love with it, too.

But Corey was gone and every time he came out here, he was painfully reminded of what might have been. Should he sell yet again and buy an apartment in the city? He knew he wouldn't want to live out there alone.

Driving through the city in the rain, he realized Pirate's race was only minutes away so he switched on to the sports racing station to follow the event. He knew Tony had high hopes of the horse, starting as a short-priced favourite today.

'And they're off!' The bell rang and the race caller started his spiel. 'The favourite, Pirate King, jumped well and is racing third behind Smooth Talk and Poppa's Hope, three lengths ahead of the rest of the field.' He went on to call the position of every horse, returning to the leaders as they rounded the final turn and spread out, taking up their positions for the run up the straight. 'Smooth Talk still out in front, Poppa's Hope gone. Elwood Red comes through to tackle Smooth Talk but here comes the favourite! Pirate King winding up on the inside next to the rail, all set to overtake both of them. But no – oh no! Elwood Red has broken down pushing Pirate King into the rail. Now the favourite is down – Pirate King and his jockey are down! Poppa's Hope recovers to take second place but Smooth Talk – Smooth Talk the outsider has held on to win by four lengths.'

Caught in traffic, Mario waited impatiently to hear what had happened to Pirate and Mercer as the place-getters were announced.

'Pirate King is up – appears to be unhurt.' The announcer reported at last, letting Mario blow out a long sigh of relief. 'But the jockey, Ray Mercer – sorry no, his replacement, Corey O'Brien, is still on the ground. Doesn't look good. She's unconscious and the ambulance men are bringing a stretcher—'

Mario hit the horn with the heel of his hand, trying to get the snarl of traffic to move. His worst nightmares had suddenly become all too real. *What was Corey doing on Pirate? Why did Ray Mercer not ride?*

He took a sharp left turn down a side street to get out of the traffic jam, pulled to the side of the road and punched Tony's number on his mobile, heart pounding. Closing his eyes, he murmured prayers to a God he suddenly believed in much more than before. He imagined the worst – spinal injury, even brain damage. Corey in traction, Corey on life-support, Corey spending the rest of her life in a wheelchair.

'Come on, Tony, come on!' he said, gritting his teeth as he waited for the trainer to answer him.

After a moment or two, Tony came on the line, sounding harassed. 'Mackintosh.'

'How's Corey?' Mario asked without preamble.

'Not too good. Still unconscious. They're taking her to the nearest emergency hospital – Dandenong.'

'I'm on my way. What the hell were you doing, Tony?' Mario needed to take his anger and anxiety out on someone and Tony was an easy victim. 'Putting Corey up on Pirate, when I specifically—?'

'Had to. Ray couldn't make the weight.'

'So why didn't you scratch?'

'Because Corey was there and happy to take him. Mario, this has nothing to do with competence – it was an accident. It can happen to anyone—'

'But it didn't happen to anyone, did it? It happened to Corey. She's so small, so—' His voice cracked and he couldn't go on.

193

'Look, mate, I know how you feel, I'm as worried as you are.' Tony sounded tense. 'Pat's going to skin me alive if anything happens to Corey. She's like a daughter to us.'

'Pity you didn't think of that before. Dandenong Hospital, is it? I'm on my way.'

Late on a Friday afternoon, the freeway was busy with trucks returning to base and vehicles clogging all lanes. Desperate to reach the hospital in record time, Mario kept changing lanes, oblivious to the blaring horns of angry drivers as he forced his way into spaces that didn't really exist. Then, on top of everything else, it started to rain.

Coming off the freeway and crossing a major road on the way to the hospital, he encountered a set of traffic lights turning yellow and didn't know whether to run them or not. Realising he would have to cross six lanes of traffic to do so, at the last moment he decided to stop. With so much else on his mind, he failed to look in the rear vision mirror and didn't see the heavily loaded truck right behind, the driver expecting him to proceed through the yellow light. It crashed into the back of the Ferrari, pushing it forward into the oncoming traffic.

Corey returned to consciousness in the emergency room, opening her eyes to see Tony and Pat, staring at her anxiously from the foot of the bed.

'Where am I?' she said, trying to sit up until the nurse who was monitoring her progress, gently pushed her down again and started taking her pulse. 'Is Pirate all right?'

'That brute will always be fine,' Tony said. 'It's you we've been worried about.'

The nurse left briefly, coming back moments later with a young doctor in tow. Tony and Pat moved away while the nurse drew the curtains around the bed for the two of them to examine and talk to Corey.

'It's good news; the x-rays show no broken bones. You're just a bit shaken up.' The doctor smiled at her when he was done. 'But as you were knocked out by the fall, you might have a mild concussion. So we'd like to keep you in for observation tonight. Fortunately, you're a strong, healthy young woman. You might be a bit bruised and sorry for yourself over the next few days but you're lucky. The baby seems to be hanging in there and unharmed.'

'*Baby*?' Corey repeated it, wondering if she'd heard him aright. 'Did you say *baby*?'

'You didn't know?' He noted her stunned expression. 'Well, it's still early days but you're having a baby – yes. This is good news, I hope?'

'Yes. No. I don't know,' Corey murmured. She had put her missing periods down to stress but now she remembered the tingling and tenderness in her breasts. *A baby!* 'It'll mean a lot of changes in my life.'

Changes that might include raising a baby alone.

'Babies always do.' The doctor smiled. 'My wife has just had twins, so I know.'

'And you're sure I'm not going to lose it because of the fall?' She folded her hands protectively over a stomach that still seemed flat as before. It was hard to believe there was new life in there.

'I don't think so. It would have happened by now. All things considered, you've had a lucky escape.'

'Thank you, Doctor.'

'Unlike the poor guy next door,' he nodded towards the next cubicle. 'Smashed himself up coming off the freeway in his Ferrari.'

'A Ferrari?' Corey's heart thudded. There weren't that many Ferraris in Melbourne. Before anyone could stop her, she was out of bed and pulling aside the curtains hiding the next patient from view. As she feared, it was Mario, lying there, eyes closed, his hair looking darker than ever against the white sheets and pillows surrounding him.

'Corey O'Brien.' The nurse caught her by the arm. 'I really must insist you get back into bed. They're ready to take you up to the ward now.'

'But I know him,' she said, desperate to stand her ground. 'We were to be married . . .'

'Darling, do as they say and get back into bed.' Gentle but firm, Pat helped the nurse steer her away. 'We'll stay here and find out what's happening to Mario. I promise to come up and tell you as soon as we know.'

Corey, who had been dry-eyed throughout the last few weeks and had not wept for her own accident, now burst into noisy, helpless tears that she couldn't control.

'Please – don't—' she managed to say between the sobs that seemed to shake her whole body. 'Don't – let anything happen – to him.'

'He'll be all right, I'm sure,' Tony said with false heartiness. 'He's a big, strong guy.'

Left to herself upstairs in the ward, Corey toyed with the

uninteresting hospital supper and considered the doctor's news as she waited for Tony and Pat to return. If she were pregnant, she would miss the spring carnival but even that didn't seem to matter now. Her anxiety for Mario was overtaking everything that had seemed so important before. Also, although bruised, she was recovering quickly and could see no reason to stay in the hospital overnight. Just as she was getting impatient enough to go downstairs again and see what was happening for herself, Pat came into the room.

'He's going to be all right,' she said, in answer to Corey's questioning gaze. 'A broken ankle and a couple of cracked ribs. Painful but not life-threatening.'

'Are you sure? He looked so – so ill and sort of lost.' Tears welled up in Corey's eyes again.

'He's a bit shaken up and still groggy with pain killers but you can see him for yourself, if I can find you something to wear.' Pat opened the cupboard opposite Corey's bed. 'You can't go running about in that hospital gown – it's all open at the back.'

'I don't care – I'll go naked, if I have to. Just tell me where he is.'

Fortunately, Pat found a dressing-gown in the cupboard and quickly wrapped it around Corey. There was no time to find out whose it was or ask their permission to borrow it. 'Now wait a moment while I get you a wheelchair—'

'I don't need a wheelchair.' Corey hopped out of bed, hitching the dressing-gown that was several sizes too big. 'Just show me where he is.'

Mario was in a private room in the same block. Corey

stood in the doorway, staring at him for a moment, shocked by the changes in this man who had always seemed so confident, so much in control of his life before. Even from here, she could see how the recent weeks had affected him, how much weight he had lost. Propped up in bed with several pillows behind him, he was wearing a hospital gown like her own. His ribs had been strapped with supportive bandages and a small cage held the bedclothes away from his broken, newly plastered foot.

'I'll leave you to it–' Pat whispered, turning to leave until Corey grabbed her arm.

'No, Pat – please don't go. It scares me to see him like this.'

'It's all right. You have a lot to discuss,' Pat said firmly. 'I'll go and find Tony – but we'll come back and see how you're doing before we leave.'

Quietly, so as not to wake him, Corey drew up a chair by the bed. In a drugged sleep, he looked still enough to be close to death. She wanted to touch his hair and his face, to see his eyes open and look into hers. She wanted to kiss that perfect mouth with forgiveness and love. No matter how she had tried to fight it, she knew that she loved him, whatever the cost. If she could only turn back the clock, she would do things differently. If he would only open his eyes and be the Mario that she knew, his old arrogant self, she wouldn't even care if he called her Rina.

Somehow, he sensed she was there and opened his eyes to squint at the light, taking a moment to take in his surroundings and focus on Corey.

'Corey!' He tried to sit up only to fall back as the pain in brandishing a single diamond engagement ring. It seemed even more dazzling in the early morning sunshine.

'I wanted you to be first to know.' Maeve hugged her, happiness making her oblivious to her sister's stunned expression. 'Jon did mention that you went out with him once or twice. It was never serious, though?'

'No.' Corey had whispered, through lips that felt suddenly numb.

*Not serious at all. If it didn't count that before meeting Maeve, Jon had slept with her at least three times a week and had promised to love her forever.*

'Darling, are you feeling all right?' Maeve's expression clouded. 'You've gone awfully pale.'

'No, no I'm just a bit tired. Wrong time of the month.' Somehow Corey swallowed the lump of misery in her throat, forced herself to smile and made all the right noises about Maeve's diamond. Drunk with happiness, Maeve chattered on.

'Jon doesn't want to wait so we're getting married quite soon. You'll have to be my chief bridesmaid.'

*Married?* She was only just getting used to the idea of their engagement. At that moment she knew she would never tell Maeve about her affair with Jon. Either she wouldn't believe it or, if she did, it would only drive a wedge between them and that would be unbearable. Corey had lost everyone else in her family, she couldn't lose Maeve as well.

So she stared at her sister's face, flushed and eyes sparkling with happiness, and smiled back, trying to give Jon the benefit of the doubt. Certainly, Maeve was the beauty of the family and maybe he was truly in love this time. At the same time, she was dreading the day she would have to stand behind her sister and watch them exchange those vows.

After the official announcement, she half-expected to hear from Jon but he gave no apology, no explanation and she heard nothing more from him until he sent her the dress he had designed to complement Maeve's bridal gown. Her first instinct was to return it but when she lifted it from its wrappings of tissue paper, she couldn't help but fall in love with the beautiful gown. A slinky dress with a plunging neckline, covered in dozens of subtle sequins of the palest moonstone blue and shimmering like the feathers of an exotic bird. Simple, yes. But incredibly elegant. And how had he so exactly remembered her size?

Somehow she got through the ceremony, the wedding party and the speeches afterwards. Jon's best man was charming and urbane but also married, his wife in hospital giving birth to their second child. Corey thought she was doing so well until, half-way through the evening, Jon crossed the room to ask her to dance. She glanced at Maeve, pink and flushed from too much champagne, presently showing off her rings to some friends. Every instinct warned Corey not to dance with him but a refusal would only cause comment and look very odd. The remembered warmth of his hand clasping hers brought hot tears to her eyes as they took to the floor.

'Mmm. Little Corey. Long time, no see.' The cliché grated on her as he looked her up and down, devouring her with his eyes. 'You look absolutely scrumptious in that dress,' he said. 'And it fits you perfectly; I knew it would.'

Corey's heart thumped with fury as much as unwanted desire. *How could he still have this effect on her?* She would have pulled free and left him standing there in the middle of the floor except that he caught her in his arms and held on, anticipating such a move.

'Let me go!' She said through gritted teeth.

'Steady on,' he said, smiling down at her. 'You're behaving like a frightened horse.'

'In case you've forgotten,' she said, struggling to keep the tremor from her voice, 'You've just made a vow of life-long fidelity to my sister.'

'Oh, I wouldn't let that worry you.' He breathed in her ear. 'People are much more relaxed about marriage, these days.'

'Maeve isn't and neither am I.' She pulled back to look him in the eye. 'We O'Briens are the old-fashioned kind.'

'Just as much of a firebrand as ever.' He ran a finger down her nose. 'Lovely Corey. I'd forgotten how pretty you are. I'm sure to find time for you.'

She would have loved to slap him hard enough to leave a mark on his face but she escaped instead. Only now did she realize she had done Maeve no favours by remaining silent about Jon. Clearly, he didn't take marriage or the vows he had made very seriously and had no intention of being a faithful husband. But it was too late to say anything now.

She had gone home and torn off the dress, intending to rip it to shreds but common sense prevailed. So instead she had buried it at the back of her wardrobe where it had remained. She had never even considered wearing it again. Until now. *Come on, Cinderella*, it seemed to be saying, *I'm exactly what you need. Choose me, tonight!*

Just then the telephone rang in the kitchen. She sprang to answer it, making sure she had pen and paper handy, expecting to take a message for Wendy.

'Corey, you're home. Good. It's Pat.'

'Hi.' Corey said softly, having recognized Pat's voice immediately and knowing what she'd have to say.

'Now come on, I know that tone.' Pat tackled the subject without preamble. 'Tony told me what happened today and I don't want you hiding at home feeling sorry for yourself. I want you here with me.'

'Oh, Pat, I don't know. If I'd won the race for you, then maybe—'

'Nonsense. We've plenty to celebrate even without a winner today.'

'Honestly Pat, I'm exhausted and I really don't have—'

'Anything to wear? Don't give me that. What about the fantastic dress you wore to Maeve's wedding?'

'I'm looking at it now. I'm not sure it's appropriate.'

'Of course it is. Look I have to go. I have a million things to do before tonight. Will you stop being sensible, down-to-earth Corey and live dangerously, for once? Take a good hot shower, followed by a cold one, put on that dress and get over here pronto. And if I don't see you within the hour, I'll send Michael to pick you up. Forget that – I'm sending him, anyway.' And before Corey could protest further, there was a soft click on the line, telling her Pat had rung off.

'Damn.' She swore softly. Now there was no way out. Michael would be here in less than an hour. Mike Mackintosh, their overgrown, eighteen year old son who had always treated her like a sister and who would delight in slinging her over his shoulder and carrying her off to the party, ready or not.

She glared at herself in the mirror and pulled a face. She looked far from inspiring, hair dull and mousy, squashed and flattened by the heat as well as the close-fitting jockey's helmet she had worn earlier that day. She had showered briefly at the track but not washed her hair. She took another shower now and conditioned her hair which sprang back obediently into its usual halo of soft reddish-blonde curls. With her skin glowing with natural good health from a life spent mostly out of doors, she needed hardly any make-up, adding only lip-gloss plus a little eyeshadow and mascara to enlarge and enhance her grey eyes.

Then it was time to wriggle into *that* dress. Yes, it still fitted perfectly, clinging to her figure like a second skin and making it impossible to wear anything underneath; even the skimpiest of panties would spoil the line. She wriggled her feet into a pair of high-heeled sandals in exactly the same shade of shimmering blue and examined the effect.

Confronted by this glamorous reflection, so unlike her boyish workaday self, she was tempted to take it all off, turn off the lights and hide under the bed when Michael came to the door. But even as she crossed her arms to take hold of the dress and pull it back over her head, the door-bell rang and Michael called out to her.

'Open up, Corey O'Brien, it's no good hiding in there. If Ma wants you at her party, it's more than my life's worth to turn up without you.'

Michael was early. He must have been in the city already when Pat diverted him. Corey opened the door, hoping to reason with him and send him away.

'*Ay Caramba*!' he said when he saw her, executing a few dance steps in the doorway. After a holiday in San Francisco and Mexico, Michael was into all things Latin American. 'You look as if you've been poured into that dress.'

'I know. It's too much, isn't it? I'll have to change.'

'No time.' Michael glanced at his watch. 'And anyway, why spoil the fun? I'm looking forward to seeing you stop the party in that.'

'I don't want to cause a sensation of any kind.' Corey's prim tone belied her appearance. 'Wait a minute while I get a shawl.'

'A shawl? What for? You'll spoil it. I think you look great as you are.' He glanced at his watch yet again. 'Come on, Corey, I've got to deliver you safely to Ma before I can pick up Josie.'

She hesitated on the doorstep and frowned, thinking of Michael's girlfriend, sulky, insecure and jealous of everyone Michael liked, even Corey who was almost a sister. 'I'm sorry, Mike. I'm ruining your evening, aren't I? Look, you go and get Josie and I'll stay home. Tell Pat I've developed a thumping headache and gone to bed.'

'You expect me to lie to my mother?' He assumed a comically shocked expression. 'Certainly not.'

Corey sighed, realizing when she was beaten, but still she made Michael wait while she found an old-fashioned Spanish shawl that had belonged to her mother. With this wrapped firmly around her shoulders, she felt a lot more secure.

In the car, Michael put some noisy Latin American music on the stereo and sat, whistling and drumming an accompaniment on the steering wheel, making conversation impossible as they sped through the suburbs and out on to the highway which would take them to Pat and Tony's new home. This was only the second time she had visited their stable complex on the outskirts of Melbourne and she hadn't yet seen inside the house. A pioneer's mansion by all accounts and rather grand. As well as a house-warming party, she knew it should also have been the celebration of Pirate's victory and Corey still felt it keenly that she hadn't been able to deliver it.

As they turned from the highway to a minor road and then into a newly made drive lined with young trees, Corey began to realize the actual size of the property and the amount of thought and capital Tony and Pat must have invested in it.

The house was a fully restored, internally modernized Federation mansion, ablaze with lights as Michael turned into the circular driveway and pulled up outside wide steps which led to an imposing double front door. A small band was already in full swing and the party well under way, making Corey feel suddenly shy and wishing she hadn't come.

But Michael sprang out of the driver's seat and ran round

to open the door for her, handing her out of the car like a lady. That was a first, as well. Had she been dressed in her old boots and riding gear, he would never have done such a thing. He'd have gone off and let her struggle out of the car on her own.

'Well, well. So, Cinderella has come to the ball after all.' It was Tony who greeted her with a kiss as they entered the hall, complete with an imposing chandelier and the obligatory bouquet of gerberas and pink liliums on a stand in front of an ornate ormolu mirror.

'But this is wonderful, Tony,' she murmured, taking in the high ceiling and impressive staircase of magnificent wrought iron and polished wood, curving away to the rooms above. 'Quite the Lord of the Manor now, aren't you?'

'Walk the walk, talk the talk,' he said, pulling a wry face. 'Needs must if we want to attract the right horses and owners.' He grinned. 'You're looking rather stunning tonight.' He glanced down at what he could see of her dress. 'But aren't you too hot in that shawl?'

'Of course she is.' Michael, who had been waiting for just such an opportunity, whisked it away. 'I'll put it upstairs in Mum's bedroom.' And he was off, galloping up the stairs two at a time before she could stop him.

'Look who's just arrived?' Tony said, winking at Pat who was also coming to greet her, dressed in a sparkling red caftan which drifted about her ample figure, making her look rather like a ship in full sail. 'Enjoy the party, Corey – catch you later – have to mingle now.'

'Corey.' Pat kissed her and then caught her by the arms,

24

swinging them wide to look at her. 'I know I've said it before but that is a fabulous dress. You look wonderful.'

'Yes but you know it's not really me—'

'Ssh! Never apologize – never explain.' Pat gave her a hug. 'You're here and that's all that matters. Now,' she put her head on one side, scanning the room. 'Who do you know already and who would you like to meet?'

'I'd like to meet her, for a start.' A tall, dark man loomed beside them. 'Never mind introducing her to anyone else.' In an impossibly well cut dinner suit which would have done credit to James Bond, he put Corey in mind of one of the larger feral cats. She recognized him immediately, catching her breath – Mario Antonello, the owner who had been so uncomplimentary about her riding skills earlier in the day.

# CHAPTER TWO

**H**IS expression was very different now. With an arm resting familiarly across Pat's shoulders, he was smiling down at her, crinkling his eyes in a way that would have devastated most girls. It might have devastated Corey, had she not still been smarting from his criticism. How stupid of her. She had forgotten that Mario, as one of Tony's newer and more prominent connections, was sure to be here.

'Come on, Pat, my love.' he was saying. 'Aren't you going to introduce me?' His gaze travelled from Corey's shoes, taking in the expensive dress and eventually settling on her lips, still parted in surprise. His voice, previously filled with scorn, was now a gentle, almost purring bass. She felt like a bird, mesmerized and about to be caught in the claws of a feral cat. 'Not a relative is she?' he continued teasing her with his eyes, although he was talking to Pat. 'I don't want Tony chasing after me with a gun.'

Pat smiled, aware that Mario hadn't recognized Corey as the jockey who had ridden Pirate for him earlier that day.

'Why, Mario,' she said sweetly, 'you've already met. Don't you recognize Corey O'Brien?'

He was good. She had to give him that. The startled look in his eyes lasted less than a moment before he recovered, taking her hand and drawing her towards him, crowding her space.

'Well, of course,' he murmured. 'How could I forget when she reminds me so much of—'

'The prize that you didn't win?' Corey put in, unable to resist the barb.

Pat, anxious to avoid a potentially bad situation, was already seeking a way to defuse it.

'Corey, my love,' she said, trying to draw her away from Mario and nodding in the direction of the buffet where she could see Tony, laughing and talking with some friends. 'Be an angel and tell Tony I need him. If I go over there, I'll get caught up in the conversation and really I haven't the time—'

'Oh no, Patricia, you're not going to take her away. Not now I've found my princess for the night.' Mario recaptured Corey's hand and pulled her towards him before she could make her escape. He was wearing a subtle but unusual cologne and his pale eyes were mesmerizing as he watched her intently through those thick dark eyelashes. In spite of her initial dislike of the man and his arrogance, Corey felt the full force of his magnetism before he turned away, murmuring to Pat, 'You can find another messenger, can't you?'

Without waiting for a reply, he steered Corey towards the ballroom where the band was playing a jazzy popular tune. As it was early, not many people were dancing. Most of the guests were still chatting or starting to pick at the buffet, leaving the floor clear.

Corey thought it best to remain cool and unimpressed by the man's charm. She would dance with him just the once and then make her escape, keeping out of his way for the rest of the night. Well, that was the plan. In a room full of so many glamorous women, he would soon attach himself to somebody else.

But as luck would have it, as soon as they reached the floor, the band stopped playing the jazzy number that would have kept them dancing just out of arm's reach. The lights went down and the mood changed as the spotlight fell on a girl singer who embarked on a medley of Harry Connick's old time favourites.

'I'm sorry, Mr Antonello. I'm really not that much of a dancer—' Corey tried once more to excuse herself but he shook his head, drawing her firmly into his embrace.

'Well I am,' he murmured. 'Just relax, listen to the music and follow me.'

Although she was petite and he was tall, her impossibly high heels made up a lot of the difference. She wasn't lying when she said she wasn't much of a dancer but it didn't seem to matter. Mario lifted her into his arms as if she had been dancing with him all her life and, after a moment or two, she closed her eyes, allowing the rhythm to take her as she breathed in that wonderful cologne, forgetting entirely that until a few moments ago she had thought of him as the enemy. A citrus scent but with all the warmth of Tuscany, soothing yet at the same time somehow disturbing, alluring even. Her eyes snapped open as she realized she ought not to be thinking such thoughts.

He smiled down at her. 'I think an apology is in order, don't you?'

Immediately, her good mood evaporated and she stiffened, almost losing the rhythm of the dance. 'What? You expect me to apologize? For losing the race?'

'Don't jump to conclusions. I mean *I* should apologize to *you* – for the way I behaved. I don't like losing, you see. It's not something I'm used to.'

She smiled, her good humour returning. 'I'm afraid you'll *have* to get used to it, if you're to survive in the racing game. For every time you find yourself in the winner's circle, there'll be many other occasions when your horse doesn't even place. They don't automatically give the same performance each time – they're not motor bikes. Thoroughbreds are living creatures with moods and minds of their own. That's what makes it so fascinating. There are no certainties in racing, Mr Antonello,' she said, echoing Tony's words.

'Mario – please,' he corrected her. As the music stopped, he led her from the floor but still didn't leave her side.

'That dress,' he said, glancing briefly at her cleavage, making her very conscious of her lack of underwear. 'It really is quite unusual. Do you mind telling me how you came by it?'

Corey stared at him, perversely tempted to say she had picked it up in a thrift shop. Why should a man be so interested in what she was wearing? He answered the unspoken question before she could speak.

'You see I understand clothes, especially Italian clothes. It's very *haute couture* – but you know that, of course. I didn't expect to see anyone wearing something like that – not at Tony's little country house gathering.'

'So what *did* you expect? To see us staggering around the dance floor with mud on our boots, wearing Drizabones?' She felt a pang of irritation at his snobbery and almost stalked off, leaving him alone on the dance floor, until he laughed and smiled into her eyes, disarming her yet again.

'Don't be so prickly. Why are you so determined to think the worst of me?' He said. 'You must have known you'd cause a sensation in that dress. It's worthy of a place on any catwalk from Paris to Milan.'

'That good, is it?' Frankly, she was surprised. Most of Jon's designs were pretty run of the mill. For a moment she was tempted to gratify his curiosity but decided against it, preferring to retain her mystery. Out of the corner of her eye, she could see Pat watching them anxiously from across the room. She tilted her head and gave Pat a broad wink to reassure her. It had the opposite effect; their hostess shrugging and raising her eyebrows as if to say *What are you up to?*

'So tell me, Corey, are you with anyone tonight?' He glanced around the room as if expecting a jealous boyfriend to materialize and whisk her away.

'With anyone?' she repeated, smiling as if she were giving the matter some careful thought. 'As it happens, no. Not tonight.'

'Good.' He said, apparently satisfied with her answer. 'I'm starving, aren't you? All that dancing has made me his ribs prevented it. 'I was listening to the race and heard what happened to Pirate. I thought you were dead.'

'So what were you doing?' she said in a shaky voice. 'Trying to get yourself killed to join me?'

He tried to laugh soundlessly until he had to stop, wincing and holding his ribs. 'It only hurts when I—'

'Laugh.' She finished the sentence for him. 'Speeding again, weren't you? Taking risks with that horrible sports car.' It was easier to rant at him rather than break down and weep her relief. 'Of all the irresponsible idiots. You're worse than a teenager. But this is the last of it. I won't have you driving that beastly machine any more.'

'No one can, anyway. It's a write-off.' He tried to keep the banter going and failed, closing his eyes against incipient tears. Suddenly serious, he caught hold of her small hand, enfolding it in both of his own. 'Corey, does this mean you still care for me? You're willing to be part of my life?' As always he found it hard to apologize, unable to put the strength of his feelings into the right words. 'I should have told you the truth about Rina from the beginning but I was too scared of losing you.' He tried to take a deep breath and ended up wincing instead. 'And then – when you found out – in the worst possible way – I lost you anyway.' He bit his lips, fighting the pain and weakness that threatened to overtake him.

She leaned forward and stroked his hair, kissing his eyelids and finally, very softly, his lips. 'You haven't lost me, Mario. You never really did.'

He opened his eyes to stare at her with those piercing blue eyes, no longer clouded with weariness. 'Can you forgive me? Will you wear your emerald for me again? And maybe – just maybe – let me buy you the wedding ring to go with it?'

She pretended to consider the matter, head on one side although really her heart was ready to burst with joy. 'I think so,' she said slowly. 'Subject to certain conditions.'

'What conditions?' he frowned, squinting at her through those impossibly thick, dark eyelashes. 'Because while we're on the subject of conditions, I have some of my own. For a start, I don't want you riding Pirate again.'

'All right.' She held up her hands in surrender. 'I promise not to ride Pirate. In fact, for the next six months, I won't ride anything but the gentlest of mares.'

Having expected contradictions and protests, this meek response left him speechless. She took advantage of it.

'And you must promise not to buy another Ferrari—'

'OK.' He shrugged.

'A Lamborghini or any other machine built for speed. You're going to need a nice, safe, solid 4WD' – and here she paused, making certain her words would sink in. 'Something more suitable for a family man.'

'Family man?' For a moment, he didn't understand. 'But I'm not—'

'Not yet. But you're going to be.' She smiled at his dawning understanding. 'In about six months.'

'Oh, Corey.' He had to embrace her then although his cracked ribs made him groan. 'This is the best news ever. My mother will be thrilled; she's wanted to be a grandmother for years. Never mind the ribs – come and kiss me properly. I love you so much.'

Just as she climbed on the bed to do so, the door was flung open and an outraged nursing sister strode into the room, hands on hips.

'So this is where you've got to, Corey O'Brien. Put that man down at once – that's bad for his blood pressure. We've been searching the hospital, looking high and low for you. And Mr Jenkins is complaining that someone has stolen his dressing gown.'

# CHAPTER TEN

The small local church was packed with invited guests. And, although Corey and Mario had tried to insist on a small, private ceremony, the churchyard was crowded with racing fans and others, meaning to catch a glimpse of the bride.

Inside, Mario waited, his cousin Bruno summoned in haste from Italy to stand beside him as best man. His mother and father were seated in a pew nearby. The minister smiled at him nervously, checking his watch and making Mario check his as well. *Ten minutes late*, he thought. *Well, that was traditional, wasn't it?*

At that moment, the organist struck up the wedding march and a murmur of approval went through the congregation as Corey appeared at the back of the church with Tony. Mario forced himself not to turn and look until she was standing there, right beside him, the bunch of white roses and freesias trembling in her hands, betraying her own nerves. For Corey, this was far more stressful than taking a thoroughbred out on to the race track.

Since Maeve was in Queensland and couldn't spare the time to come back, she had dispensed with the tradition of having a bridesmaid. Now, in the process of managing flowers and veil on her own, she was beginning to wish she had one.

At last she looked up at Mario, standing tall beside her, knowing that she could depend on him for the rest of her life. He smiled down at her, his eyes telling her all that she needed to know and she smiled back. This was her day and she was suddenly no longer troubled by nerves.

Tony, having delivered the bride to the altar, took his seat beside Pat.

'She's looking lovely today,' he murmured. 'Radiant as a bride should be. Brilliant idea of yours to lend her your mother's wedding dress.'

'What else would I do with it?' Pat whispered, smiling ruefully. 'I showed it to Josie once and she said she wouldn't be seen dead in such an old-fashioned gown. But it's perfect for Corey – suits her colouring, too. Cream silk and hand-made lace from the nineteen thirties. They made dresses to last in those days.' She looked at the bride and groom quietly making their responses and let go a long sigh.

'What is it now, love?' Tony whispered. 'Something's eating you.'

'I hope they'll be all right – he isn't marrying her just because of the baby?'

'Oh, I don't think so.' Tony laughed softly at the idea. 'That sort of thing used to happen in our day. But not now. And if you don't believe me just look at the man. Head over heels in love.'

203

'I don't know, Tony. He didn't buy her a wedding present. Traditional, that is. Corey showed me the beautiful gold watch that she was giving him yesterday. But far as I know, she's had nothing at all from him.'

'Far as *you* know.' Tony smirked.

'Tony Mackintosh!' She pinched him sharply, making him wince and rub his arm. 'What do you know that I don't?'

Outside the church, they all posed for photographs, as this was traditional, too. Corey threw her bouquet, making certain that Josie would catch it, laughing when Michael frowned at her and blushed, shaking his head.

'Thanks a lot, Corey O'Brien. I'll get no peace now,' he muttered.

The reception, given by Pat and Tony, was at their house. They had engaged the same band which had played at their house-warming party, less than a year before.

As Corey danced the bridal waltz with her husband, she marvelled that so much could happen in such a short space of time. When she had danced to this band before, she had no thought in her mind but making a name for herself at the track. Now she was married and about to become a mother as well. And that was wonderful – it was what she wanted. But did it mean she would have to give up all her dreams for the future?

'Penny for them?' Mario whispered. 'You were looking a bit pensive?'

'I was thinking how much can change in such a short time.'

'Are you feeling all right?' He looked around at their

guests who were now joining them on the floor. 'Now we've got them started, we can sit this one out.'

As soon as they sat down, people crowded around to offer congratulations and talk to them. Time passed quickly and soon it was time for Corey to change from her wedding finery ready for 'going away.' Mario had been secretive about their destination but had warned her to dress comfortably so she was expecting a journey by plane.

Both Pat and Mario's mother shed a few tears as they said their good-byes and in no time at all were heading out on to the highway in their brand new Volvo. Mario had been stubborn, refusing to be bullied into driving a 4WD. 'Hard sprung, uncomfortable things,' he complained. 'Besides, I have no intention of driving over rough ground. Let's go for a little luxury for once in our lives.'

And Corey admitted she was grateful for the well-sprung comfort of the sedan.

But instead of taking the freeway to the airport as she expected, Corey realized Mario had turned on to one of the highways heading north.

'We're not going by plane, then?' She sat forward, looking out of the window.

'Not good for the baby. You're over four months now,' he said.

'So we're driving to Sydney?'

'No,' he said, still secretive, shaking his head.

'Where, then?'

'You'll have to wait and see.'

And as he would say no more and Corey was exhausted after the wedding and the reception, she fell asleep, her head on his shoulder, breathing in the familiar scent of his Tuscan cologne. She was unaware of the car climbing the winding mountain road and didn't wake until she heard it leave the open road, wheels crunching on the stones of a driveway. She sat up and peered out of the window, trying to see where they were.

'A farmhouse bed and breakfast? How lovely,' she said, although she was a little surprised when nobody came to greet them and Mario had a key to unlock the front door.

'A friend of yours has lent us this place for our honeymoon?' she tried again, but still Mario shook his head. 'They've left us supper as well, I can smell it.' She said, opening the door to the kitchen. 'And look at that – a table and chairs exactly like the ones in your kitchen at the "museum".'

'Mm.' He nodded. 'Fancy that.'

'What a lovely house. I can't wait to see it in daylight. How long can we stay?'

Mario shrugged, smiling at her. 'It's dark now but tomorrow I'll show you the stables.'

'Stables?' She brightened immediately. 'They have horses here?'

'Not yet. But the place will he humming quite shortly. Imported mares.'

'Like yours and Tony's?'

'Uhuh.' He pulled out a chair for her at the table. 'You must be starving. Sit down and let's have supper, shall we?'

He opened the big, old-fashioned oven and, with mittens provided nearby, took out a fish pie, sizzling in a heavy French pot, and placed it carefully on a stand in the middle of the table.

'How lovely,' she said, holding the rail of the old-fashioned stove. 'We had an Aga out there in the country when
I was growing up. I've always wanted one. The warm heart
of a country home.'

He nodded and smiled, finding some cutlery in a drawer
and some plates in a cupboard.

'You seem to know your way around this house. You've
been here before?'

'Uhuh.'

'Mario, stop it. You've said nothing but "Mm" and "uhuh"
all night.'

'So eat your supper. Then I'll show you over the rest of
the house.'

She was hungry enough to do justice to a delicious,
curried fish pie, trying to remember where she had tasted
one like it before.

'I'm not opening the champagne until you've had your
tour of the house.' Mario held out his hand to lead her.

She loved the family room with the huge, stone open
fireplace but couldn't help feeling the bookshelves and
furniture seemed vaguely familiar. She was about to say so
when Mario hurried her on, opening a door on a small
sitting room with doors that opened on to a patio with a
small walled garden beyond.

Mario passed what must be a bathroom and other
bedrooms to show her the master bedroom at the far end of
the ranch-style farmhouse. Inside was a huge, king-sized
bed and hanging on the opposite wall was a picture she
recognized.

'Your Klimt?' she said. 'Your special print from the

gallery. How does that come to be here?' He started smiling
and then laughed as he saw she was struck by a thought so
stunning, she could scarcely believe it. 'Mario, stop teasing
and tell me – who does this house belong to?'

'You like it? Really like it? Because if not we can always
sell—'

'Don't you dare. I adore it. When are we moving in?'

'We already have. Take a look at your walk-in wardrobe.'

Still not quite believing him, Corey opened the door and
went in. 'Mario! My clothes, my boots and shoes, they're all
here. But when I left this morning to go to Pat's house to get
dressed, they were still in the flat . . .'

'Mike got a friend with a van to bring everything over. It
was Josie's job to make sure you didn't go back to the flat
and spoil the surprise.' He was suddenly solemn. 'I know
I've done all this without asking you, being high-handed
again. Did I do the right thing?'

'Yes, oh yes.' She jumped into his arms, light and tiny
enough to wrap her legs around his hips. 'I love everything
about it, especially you.'

'Then welcome home, Mrs Mario Antonello.'

ravenous. I'm sure we could do justice to Pat's supper.'

About to murmur her excuses and head for the bath-room, she caught sight of Michael's girlfriend, Josie, glaring at her – and the dress – from a position near the door. In no mood to tangle with Josie who was looking more sullen than ever, eyes thickly ringed in kohl and wearing a minis-cule dress of black leather, Corey accepted the offer of supper and wriggled her fingers at Josie whose scowl only deepened.

'Champagne?' Mario said smoothly, capturing two glasses from a tray on the bar.

'Oh no, not really, I have to watch—'

'Your figure? Don't give me that.' Once more his gaze flickered over her dress. 'It's perfect. If you'd been a few inches taller, you could have been a model.'

'A model? Me?' Corey laughed at the idea. 'I don't think so. Anyway, I'm perfectly happy doing what I do.'

'Are you?' Mario's smile faded. 'Competitive racing is a dangerous occupation – far too dangerous for a woman.'

'On the wrong day, it can be dangerous for anyone – man or woman.' Once more she found herself irritated by his attitude. To quell her temper, she took a mouthful rather than a sip of champagne and almost coughed.

'Not used to it, are you?' He smiled as she struggled not to sneeze as the bubbles went up her nose. 'You really are Cinderella. In her fabulous gown.'

'Then you'd better call me the Princess Crystal,' she said, going along with the joke.

'And will you vanish in a puff of smoke when the clock strikes midnight, leaving me with your shoe?'

'Probably,' she giggled. On an empty stomach, the champagne was going to her head and, in spite of her earlier misgivings, she was beginning to like him.

Over supper they discovered they shared a passion for seafood, arguing over the best way to serve oysters.

'Fresh oysters served with a squeeze of lemon – they need nothing more,' he insisted.

'Yes but if you add a touch of chili sauce to the lemon, it gives them an extra zing,' she told him.

After the oysters they shared a huge crayfish with some salad, leaving no room for Pat's famous trifle or any other dessert.

During the course of the evening they danced again and Mario politely but firmly resisted attempts by anyone to cut in. On several occasions, Pat and then Tony tried to lure her away but each time Mario headed them off refusing to let her go. And to her own surprise she was enjoying herself far too much to object. Midnight came and went, the signal for most of the older guests to leave but they stayed on together and at 2 a.m. Corey, drinking coffee, stifled a yawn.

'You're tired,' he said, surprisingly attentive to her needs. 'This has been a long day for you. Let me drive you home.'

'Oh no, there's no need, I have my own—' Then she paused, biting her lip as she remembered her own car wasn't waiting outside because Michael had collected her from the city. It seemed hardly fair to expect Mike to take her all the way back to town again – and Josie would be far from amused.

As if conjured by her thoughts, Michael appeared at her

32

side, shawl in hand which he dropped around her shoulders before saluting her.

'Mum's orders. Mike Mackintosh reporting for taxi duty. Unless of course you'd rather stay the night? Welcome any time, as you know.'

For a moment, she was tempted by the offer. But did she really want the evening to end so abruptly? This was the first time in a year that she had been able to relax and enjoy herself without being tormented by memories of Jon and his perfidy. If she stayed, Mario would leave and that would be the end of it.

'It's sweet of you Mike,' she said at last. 'But you're in luck. Mario has offered to drive me home.'

'Mario?' Michael repeated, looking from one to the other. 'Oh, really? But Mum said you were—'

'In need of rescue from the big bad wolf?' Mario said smoothly. 'No. You can assure her that the Princess Crystal will be perfectly safe with me.'

'The Princess—?' Michael was looking more and more perplexed. 'Will somebody please tell me what's going on?'

'Mikie!' This came as a shriek from Josie. 'What are you doing? The olds and that dreadful band have gone home. We can have some decent music on the stereo now. Are you coming or not?'

'Michael, go.' Corey whispered, urging him towards Josie. 'Honestly, I'm fine.'

'Well, if you're sure.' Still not entirely happy, Michael allowed his girl friend to drag him away. Corey thought of finding Pat and Tony to say goodbye but they were deep in conversation with people she recognized as new owners and this wasn't the time to intrude. She would ring Pat and thank her properly in the morning.

Outside, the night was clear and a light breeze was now blowing off the sea, bringing relief to what might otherwise have been a hot summer night. Unused to drinking alcohol of any kind, much less champagne, the fresh air made Corey feel slightly dizzy as Mario steered her towards his car. What else would it be but a silver Ferrari Modena, so perfect for him it was almost a cliché. A machine built for speed, suave and sleek as the man himself, totally out of place among the mud-covered Range Rovers and other more horse-oriented vehicles.

Once more she hesitated. Was this wise? What did she know of this man except he was a wealthy client of Tony and Pat? Maybe she should have accepted their offer to stay the night? But if she had, she would still have needed a lift back to the city in the morning. Too late to change her mind now.

Inside, the car smelled of expensive, new leather, the passenger seat so laid back that she found herself lying almost full length on the floor of the car. Feeling vulnerable and awkward in this position, she struggled to alter it and Mario leaned across to help her do so. When the seat had been adjusted to a more upright position and the seat-belt clasped firmly in place, his face was suddenly very close to her own. For a second or two she studied him, wide-eyed, still able to catch a whiff of that devastating cologne. The man was more rugged than really good-looking, his nose too large and his jawline too wide and square to make him conventionally handsome. And although he must have started the evening clean shaven, a dark shadow was showing through at this late hour, giving him a slightly menacing air. Suddenly, she was very much aware that this was a man she was dealing with, not a boy.

Tall and athletic in build, he exuded charm and confidence, certain of his ability to attract any woman. So why on earth should he be so interested in her? It made no sense. And he had been married as well, she reminded herself, and might very well expect a lot more from the end of this evening than she was prepared to give. So why? *Why* was she getting all this attention when there had been no shortage of lovely, unattached women at Tony's party? During the course of the evening, she had given him more than one opportunity to make his excuses and leave. Instead he had remained at her side all night.

For a second or two, it seemed as if time stood still, the moment lengthening as he gazed deeply into her eyes as if he would read her soul. But before the moment became uncomfortable, he smiled and broke the silence, trailing one finger gently down her cheek to pause at the corner of her mouth.

'You don't have to be scared of me, Princess.' He said softly. 'I'm quite civilized. I don't bite.'

'Who's scared?' She shrugged, unwilling to let him see how much his nearness disturbed her. 'I've never been scared of anyone in my life.'

'Lucky you,' he said softly, almost to himself. Her reactions were so like Rina's, it was uncanny. Unbelievable, wonderful, almost like having her back. Who would blame him for revelling in it, even if it was just for this one night?

He put the key in the ignition and the car started immediately with an obedient growl. He eased it slowly down the drive, making the least amount of noise so as not to disturb the valuable horseflesh, stabled nearby.

On reaching the highway, he accelerated into the fast lane, pressing one or two buttons on the console so that beautiful music surrounded them. Classic Italian opera – what else? Yet another cliché. But Corey didn't mind, happy to sit back and enjoy the ride.

'You like opera?' he asked her after a while.

She looked across at him and smiled. 'I won't pretend to understand all of it – I don't speak Italian. But somehow it seems very suitable here – tonight.' Satisfied with her answer, he smiled in return and they continued their journey in companionable silence, accompanied by soaring voices and the familiar, well-loved melodies of *La Boheme*.

She wasn't sure if she dozed or merely went into a trance with the music but in no time at all, he was asking for directions as they followed the highway, meandering through the suburbs alongside the beach. Moments later they pulled up outside the old-fashioned apartment block she called home.

'You must have a wonderful view,' he said, looking back over his shoulder. 'I'd like to see it.' He couldn't have made it more plain that he expected to be invited in.

She ignored the hint, fumbling with the door handle in her haste to get out of the car. 'Thank you, Mario. I had a great time tonight. And thanks for driving me home.'

'And that's it, is it?' He raised his eyebrows, clearly unused to being brushed off in this way. 'No *come in for coffee, Mario*? And I could murder an early breakfast.' He glanced at his watch. 'It's almost time.' He switched off the engine and gave her a bright smile. 'Car's going to be all right here, isn't it?' He peered around looking for parking infringement warnings. 'Not likely to get towed away?'

Corey looked at him, once more at a loss for something to say. Fortunately, she had no riding engagements that day – she would have had to cancel them anyway, after drinking all that champagne. Mario Antonello was a dangerous prospect in more ways than one; he had already led her astray.

'Look Mario, I don't think so.' She said at last. 'Please don't think it's because I didn't enjoy your company – I really did but I—'

'Ah,' he said, sitting back and nodding as he reached the wrong conclusion. 'I should've guessed. You have a boyfriend? You don't live here alone?'

It would have been the easiest thing in the world to say 'yes' and let it go at that but the devil sitting on Corey's shoulder all evening refused to let it end that way. It spoke up before her sensible self could prevent it. 'No, I haven't a boyfriend at present. My flatmate is a girl – she works on the airlines.'

'And she's sleeping now and you think we should disturb her?'

'No.' Corey smiled, thinking of the many nights she had lost sleep because of Wendy and her party-loving friends. 'But it is kinda late and I have to—'

'Work in the morning? Don't princesses ever take the day off? I'm sure jockeys do.' He teased. 'I won't stay more than five minutes, I promise. Just long enough to get a strong coffee and stretch my legs. You wouldn't want me to fall asleep driving home?'

'No, of course not,' she said, feeling ashamed at her lack of hospitality. 'How far is home?'

He shrugged, allowing her to think it could be some distance away.

'Just five minutes, then.' She knew she sounded less than gracious. But if Wendy wasn't back, she'd be in the apartment with him alone and she wasn't quite sure she was ready for that. He seemed to have no such concerns.

'Nice place,' he commented, following her inside. She was very much aware of his presence close behind her as they moved through the hall and she switched on the lights in the lounge. The room was a mess and she wished she'd taken the time to clear up before she went out. She moved around swiftly now, picking up newspapers and plumping cushions on the couch. 'Don't bother with that,' he said, catching her hand. 'A little untidiness makes a place more like home.'

The touch of his hand surprised her with a jolt almost like electricity. It was only the smallest of gestures and meaningless in itself but somehow hugely significant, making her very conscious of his nearness, his hand much warmer than her own.

'I'll put the coffee on.' She felt herself blushing as he held on to her hand just a little longer than necessary.

'Such a hard little hand.' He turned it over to examine the calloused palm. 'From riding, of course. I must say it keeps you fit. When we were dancing earlier, I felt the strength in your thighs.'

Corey felt more and more disconcerted. Was he out to seduce her? Now he was mentioning thighs! She was far from innocent – certainly not after Jon – but he had never commented on hands, thighs or any other body parts. Quickly, she made her escape, murmuring about coffee.

In the kitchen, she viewed her reflection in the mirror next to the fridge pressing her hands to her flushed cheeks. Too much party, too much to drink and certainly too much Mario. Rejecting her own bottle of 'instant,' she searched the cupboards for Wendy's exotic American brand and filled the drip-filter machine before setting a tray with milk and sugar. They had no expensive china so she had to use mugs. At least they were Denby.

When it was ready she brought it in to find him standing up, studying the various family portraits on the mantelpiece, mainly her own. There was a picture taken on Maeve's wedding day, Jon beside her and Corey, behind them, wearing the blue dress. No more mystery, then. Her secret was out.

'Jon Manolito,' he murmured. 'Of course. I should have recognized his hand in this.'

'In what?' Corey said, puzzled.

Mario ignored the question, posing one of his own instead. 'Pretty girl, his wife. Friend of yours?'

'My sister.' Corey answered him briefly, unwilling to discuss Maeve or the complications of their relationship. 'Now,' she said brightly, changing the subject. 'How do you like your coffee?'

'Black. And I hope you made it strong enough?' He plumped a cushion and flung himself down on the couch, getting ready to make himself at home.

'The spoon will stand up in it if it gets any stronger. And don't make yourself too comfortable – five minutes, remember?'

'Why? Am I making you nervous?' He grinned, accepting the mug she held out to him. 'A decent sized cup too. I hate those nasty little things my mother uses. Too easy to drop.'

Although the coffee must have been scalding, he finished it quickly and immediately stood up to leave. Corey followed him to the door, surprised to experience mixed feelings yet again. On the one hand there was relief that he had decided against making a move on her. On the other, she was sorry that this magical evening was finally at an end.

But before she could open the front door he turned and faced her, giving her a searching look and shaking his head.

'Such a strange girl. Full of contradictions,' he said, running a finger down her bare arm and making her shiver. 'One moment I feel that you like me and the next you back off like a startled fawn, hiding behind your barriers once again. From the outset you knew I was intrigued with that dress – so why didn't you tell me your sister was married to Manolito?'

'I don't know.' Corey shrugged, avoiding his gaze. Any mention of Jon made her uncomfortable. 'Perhaps because it was none of your business.'

'There you go again.' He said, his expression clouding. 'Putting me firmly in my place. And just as I was hoping we could be friends.'

'But why me? I'm not beautiful, not special, not even brainy. I don't know much about anything except horses.'

*Oh, you're special all right*, he thought. *Creeping into my heart and reminding me so much of Rina, it almost hurts. Every time I look at you, I feel as if she's back in my life again; as if I never lost her at all.* But of course he couldn't say that. No girl likes to be compared to a former love. That's what had driven Anna away in the end. *'I won't compete with a ghost,'* she had said.

'All right,' he said. 'At first I was intrigued with the dress. It bears an uncanny resemblance to the "mermaid" line we created in Italy last season.'

'And you're saying Jon copied it?'

'No,' he laughed shortly. 'Even if he had, it would be extremely hard to prove and probably not worth the effort.'

'Nothing would surprise me about Jon.'

'Oh? You don't have a high opinion of your brother-in-law?'

For a moment, she thought of confiding in him until she realized how lame it must sound; that Jon dumped her to marry her sister and then hit on her at his own wedding reception. Something so crass, so unbelievable, he would have to think she was making it up. She still felt a weight of guilt that she hadn't found the courage to tell Maeve the truth. Jon was clearly a cheat in more than one arena. Instead she shrugged her shoulders and sighed.

Mario looked at her. Suddenly, she seemed small, vulnerable and in need of comfort, her expression anxious with tired hollows beneath her eyes. And before she realized what he would do, he had gathered her into his arms,

41

surprising her with a kiss before she could draw breath to say anything more.

Hands pressed against his chest, she tensed against him, afraid the kiss might not be to her liking. Raised among stable hands, she was used to protecting herself from impulsive kisses and clumsy advances. Jon hadn't been much better; his kisses demanding and invasive, always driving towards the fulfilment of sex. But Mario's was quite different; gentle and teasing at first, yet building slowly to a passion until a delicious heat invaded her body as if every nerve had been coaxed alive. He still smelled vaguely of that lemony, Tuscan aftershave and masculine good health and tasted of Wendy's good coffee. After a moment or so, she couldn't help but respond, closing her eyes as she sighed and relaxed against him, winding her arms about his neck and kissing him back.

'Hmm,' he said softly, dropping a final kiss on her head as he disengaged himself to open the door. 'A pleasing beginning, after all. Now you sleep well, Cinderella. I'll be in touch.' And with that he was gone, leaving her momentarily stunned, staring at the space he had occupied only moments before.

'No. No Mario, wait—' She called after him as she ran down the steps to catch up with him to say there was no point in calling because she couldn't see him again. She wasn't in love with Jon any more – far from it – but even after all this time she felt emotionally battered and bruised, not yet ready to embark on a new relationship.

But having deciding to leave, Mario moved faster than she did. She reached the kerb only in time to hear the growl of the Ferrari and catch the red glimmer of tail lights as it disappeared around the corner at the end of the street.

*Fool*, she told herself. *Just as well you didn't catch up with him. What were you thinking? Of course 'I'll be in touch' didn't mean anything. It was just a convenient thing to say – a way to leave without committing himself. A man like that must have dozens of girls at his beck and call. Why should he want to see you again?*

She went to bed in the hope of getting some rest but her mind was far too busy to let her sleep, replaying everything they had said and done. Was it possible to fall in love in the space of one night? In hindsight, apart from kissing him soundly before he left, her own behaviour had been off-hand and far from encouraging. If she didn't hear from him, she'd have no one to blame but herself. And how would she feel about that? Let down? Disappointed?

At last she gave up all hope of sleep, showered and went for an early morning jog on the beach, hoping the sea breezes would clear her mind as well as her head.

When she got back she found Wendy sitting at the kitchen table in front of a pot of fresh coffee, her long dark hair scraped up and pulled back dramatically, held in place with a clip shaped like an artificial tiger-lily. Even in a dressing gown with scarlet tipped fingers clasped around a mug, Wendy still managed to look sophisticated and immaculately groomed.

'How disgustingly healthy,' she said, wrinkling her nose at Corey who was still breathing heavily, flushed and perspiring after her run. 'Jogging on the beach at dawn.'

'I needed to blow the cobwebs away.' Corey grinned back

at her. 'Have a good trip?'

'Nothing memorable.' Wendy raised her eyes heaven-wards and sighed. 'Boring old business men in first class – noses buried in *The Financial Times*. And as for the crew – all the good-looking ones seem to be married these days – can't wait to show you their baby pictures. People think flying is glamorous but it's not. It's just a grind like any other job. What you do is far more interesting and unusual. Ride any winners yesterday?'

Corey shook her head. She didn't feel like explaining about her near miss. 'Wendy, while I think of it, I pinched some of your coffee last night. I'll replace it as soon as I can get to the—'

'Absolutely no need.' Wendy waved her protests away. 'It's cheap as chips where I get it from. But I saw the two mugs on the coffee table. So,' she said, raising a perfect eyebrow. 'Does this mean Corey has a new man in her life? Or did Sandy's brother finally—?'

'Sandy's brother was always a non-starter – I told you. And no, I don't have a new man – just a ship that passed in the night.'

'A very rich ship, then.' Wendy held out a gold cuff link, set with a large diamond, flashing as it caught the light. 'Look what I found under the cushion on the couch. If that's a diamond it has to be worth at least a grand.'

'Really?' Corey spoke casually but her heart was singing. Now he would *have* to come back; she would see him in daylight, without the added glamour of evening clothes. Then she might find it easier to decide if these new feelings were random or real. 'It's probably just a rhinestone.'

'Get serious.' Wendy gave her a pitying glance. 'Men don't wear rhinestones. What sort of car does he drive?'

'A silver one.'

'Yeah, yeah.' Wendy clicked her fingers, impatient with the joke.

'A Ferrari Modena.'

'I rest my case.' A calculating look came into Wendy's eyes.

'And you don't have to look like that. I'm not even sure I want to see him again.'

'Good. Can I have him then?'

'No.'

'Hah – so you *are* interested. And it's about time. Honestly Corey, you can't spend the rest of your days pining for that miserable rat who married your sister—'

'I'm not. I'm so over Jon, I can't even be bothered to despise him. But I'm not sure I'm ready to take up with somebody new.'

'Then you better get ready and be quick about it. Corey – hello!' Wendy leaned towards her, waving a hand in front of her face. 'You've actually snagged a rich boyfriend – you should be over the moon. Unless he's got dog's breath and a face like the back of a bus?'

Ruefully Corey shook her head. ' 'Fraid not. He's an absolute dish. George Clooney with a dash of Harvey Keitel.'

'Now, I'm really intrigued.' Wendy patted the seat beside her. 'You'd better sit down and tell Momma all about it.'

'Wouldn't you rather open your mail?' Stalling for time, Corey offered Wendy a pile of envelopes that had accumulated while she was away.

'They'll keep.' Wendy pulled a face. 'Probably only bills. Stop trying to change the subject and give.'

Over coffee and with a lot of prompting from Wendy, Corey told everything, starting with Mario's outburst at the races, Pat's insistence that she should be at the party and the magical evening that followed.

'So which is the real Mario?' she sighed. 'The sore loser I met at the track or the man I spent the evening with last night?'

'Who cares?' Wendy shrugged. 'I wouldn't stress on it. I know about rich boyfriends; they get bored very easily. Don't expect it to last. Just grab all the presents and make the most of it while you can.'

'Wendy, that's dreadful. Gold digging.'

'No. Jus' being practical, darlin.' A man like that is goin' to give presents to someone – might as well be you.' Suddenly, Wendy was all business. 'We need a plan of action. What will you say when he calls? Don't wanna sound too eager. Better hang back a bit an' let him make all the running—'

As if on cue the telephone rang, making them both jump and stare at it in surprise.

'You don't suppose—?' Wendy put her hand over her mouth and giggled.

'That's not funny.' Corey glared at her and picked it up gingerly as if it might bite, answering with a cautious – 'Yes?'

'Corey, is that you?' It was Pat Mackintosh on the line. 'You sound a bit wary? Expecting a call from the tax man?'

46